2nd Place

A Story of Hope

By Cameron P. Clark

authorHOUSE

AuthorHouse™
1663 Liberty Drive
Bloomington, IN 47403
www.authorhouse.com
Phone: 1-800-839-8640

© *2010 Cameron P. Clark. All rights reserved.*

No part of this book may be reproduced, stored in a retrieval system, or transmitted by any means without the written permission of the author.

First published by AuthorHouse 11/3/2010

ISBN: 978-1-4520-5559-6 (sc)
ISBN: 978-1-4520-5560-2 (hc)
ISBN: 978-1-4520-5561-9 (e)

Library of Congress Control Number: 2010912665

Printed in the United States of America

This book is printed on acid-free paper.

Photo of Cameron Clark courtesy of WildRoseImages.net
Cover Illustration by William Francis O'Brien
Concept Editing by Lorena Hamon Rodgers
Proof Editing by Janice Leavitt Clark

Because of the dynamic nature of the Internet, any Web addresses or links contained in this book may have changed since publication and may no longer be valid. The views expressed in this work are solely those of the author and do not necessarily reflect the views of the publisher, and the publisher hereby disclaims any responsibility for them.

For Jamie

Chapter 1: 1981–1982

Chapter 1: 1981-1982

June 3rd, 1981

I am very happy today because it is my ate-th birthday. Four my birthday I got a new bike. We moved to ~~are~~ our new house today. I hope I like my new school. I will miss my friends from our old school in Dallis. This is my journal that I am sposed to keep. Mom toled me it will be fun to read this when I am older.

September 4th, 1981

Mom says that she wants to help me get better in writing and she will cross out words I make wrong, and then we figure out what to put instead of the ~~crost~~ crossed out words. She said sometimes she will leave words if they look cute or funny. We had a fun time at the new school. My favorite class is Jim. Mom wants me to be in choir. I ~~sayed~~ said no. She ~~putted~~ got me in anyway. I don't like it really good. My real teacher is Miss Berry. She is ~~betterer~~ better than my old teacher at ~~Dallis~~ Dallas because she is way funner. She tells stories and reads us books that we like.

December 12, 1981

Mom says I get to stay up late only for if I write something in my journal. She wishes I would write in this more times. Tonight we all sang in our choir ~~consert~~ concert it sounded ~~prity~~ pretty good she said. It was fun to see dad and mom both be able to show up and hear us sing. The concert was at the come unity hall. I never went ~~their~~ there before tonight. Mom says to sleep now. Zzzz

2nd Place

April 3, 1982

    I made a new best friend today– Eddy Talent. He moved here later than me. His family is sad cause the dad went to live in a different town for some reason. Eddy thinks it is because his dad got too tired of having to babysit when his mom went to play bingo. I like bingo. I wish we played it more at my house cause mom always gives us ~~exter~~ extra treats of chocolate, and I always win those kind. Anyway, Eddy can run real fast. I was the fastest kid in class until he came. I will still be his friend though because he is nice even if he wins races outside in the playground.

Chapter 2: 1983-1984

Chapter 2: 1983-1984

September 17, 1983

    Mom said I should write more in my journal after watching Six-Million Dollar Man. She is sad cause I didn't ~~right~~ write in my journal for over a year she says I should tell more than a one paragraph for today and I will need to talk about the stuff from last year at school when I went for track and field. Eddy is still living at my school and is my friend still and he won the 50 yard dash against me and the whole class. I tried my hardest and even started better ~~then~~ than Eddy because he wasn't watching the starter guy as good as me. I didn't cry when I lost because dad was at the races, and he hates crying and I wanted to still get a big gulp for racing my hardest. Mom says that I ~~writed~~ wrote enough today. My favorite part of the day is when she stands by my bed each night, and asks me to tell her all of the stuff I did that day before I fall asleep.

September 18, 1983

    Mom says I should talk more about music, since she is paying lots of money for my piano lessons I hate having to learn over and over the same songs. My teacher at piano thinks that I am lazy but I know I'm not because I can beat her in a race any day. When no body watches me I can play the piano ~~rilly~~ really good with not even looking at the books I can play old Mac Donald farm and Three blind mice. I kind of got use to choir and don't hate it as bad as last year. We got a new leader lady and she always picks the funner kind of songs that kids like to sing louder and softer. I think her name is Mrs. Burwell. She smiles way more than ~~are~~ our other teacher because I think her new boyfriend tells better jokes. He comes to all of the concerts and gives her flowers and chocolates one time Mrs. Burwell even gave me one when no body else was looking at me. My hand is tired and I hope mom likes how long I said stuff about music.

October 3, 1983

I was all alone when I came home from school today because mom and dad are in the hospital together for when my little brother gets born. Grandma Workman is helping me write today because she is here and dad says I need to take care of her in case she gets older while I am here. She put on her special glasses and readed my journal so far and she laffed a kuppel of times because of stuff I said when I was much littler. She toled me that I need to say my whole name because so far I only writed about my friends and teachers and no one knows my name or my mom and dad's name yet. My name is Ricky Aaron Workman my dad's name is Jonathon Edward Workman and mom's name when she was little was Sarah Jane Palmer and my new little brother is not got a name yet until mom and dad finely decide who he looks like in the family and then they will pick a name that is close to the same as that guy.

October 5, 1983

I think it is not fun to have a baby in the house with us. I can't wait until he grows up. My little baby brother is so little always smells like he just barely puked again. Mom and dad are still picking between too 2 two names because he looks like too many people in the family that are already dead but we have pictures of those guys. I hope they don't call him Cleon because that is a funny sounding name for a baby.

Chapter 2: 1983-1984

That was my grate grampas name for his whole life he got teased I think. Well I don't know for sure but I do know I would tease a kid if that were his real name. Mom says I have to fix my own mistakes for a few times in my journal cause she is busy feeding the baby. I think it is a good thing that mommys have two bumps on their chest because it gives a baby a place to rest their head while the mommy feeds him with a bottle and if the mom's one arm gets tired she can always switch to the other side too. Maybe that is the reason moms are made that way by God. I think their will not be any mistakes in my writing anymore because my teacher says I am the best at language at my class. I got a VG on my last report card for language. I also got that for music and fizz ed. It is funny that it is called that because when I first heard that I thought it was a class to learn how to make pop to drink. The school in Dallas just called it Jim even though the teacher's name was not really Jim I think it was Dave in sted.

    We learned to make a new paragraph in language today so I am going to make that one right here since I will be talking about a new thing now for this journal. I got so mad today when I didn't get picked up on time to play in our football game. I was not able to get to the bus at the right time because of my piano lesson I want to quit so much because my teacher doesn't like me cheating and playing without the book all the time. Eddy got to go and he played more because I wasn't there. I told mom that I will quit trying my best in piano if she is ever late to help me get to football again.

October 12, 1983

    Today I got to go to Eddy's birthday party. We got to eat lots of treats and play games like pin the tail on the donkey. Eddy got a Steve Largent jersey from his dad. Steve Largent plays for Seattle Seahawks I think. I wish I could get a jersey like that someday. Maybe only dads that leave their kids are the only kind of dad that can afford to buy a nice jersey like that. Eddy's Dad still lives a long way from here. I think it is better for my dad to stay with us because mom has been extra sick lately because the baby makes her stay up late every night. When mom gets extra sad dad will bring her flowers home on his way from work he stops at her favorite store and she always gives him a big hug and I have to leave the room when she kisses him because I don't like to watch that too well.

December 25, 1983

    I got some new shoes for sports, a Nintendo with Donkey Kong, and a bunch of clothes for Christmas. I think that underwear is kind of a cheep present for Santa Claus to bring because everybody needs that and Christmas presents are supposed to be more for fun stuff. I am happy I got Donkey Kong even though it is an old game.

    Mom says we should be greatful for what we get from Santa because he knows if we like it or not and we never want to hurt his feelings. Mom shore knows a lot about Santa. She says she is won of the only people who knows his real phone number. I don't think Santa has a phone because I looked at the world ball in science class and there are no towns on top of the world on the white part. Maybe the

Chapter 2: 1983-1984

north pole is made from the kind of tower my grampa has. He calls it his ham radio, even though we don't eat it. Grandpa Workman says he can talk to people anywhere else in the world if they have a ham radio too. I think it would be way better if they just use the thing that Captain Kirk uses on Star Trek. I hope I have one of those someday. That would be a really cool present for Christmas.

May 8, 1984

Today was the races at school. I really wanted to win for a change. Eddy doesn't really have to try his hardest. He is just so fast. Every day in April I went running after supper to practice for these races. Dad told me that it would make my legs and lungs more used to it.

The only happy news from today is that I had the fastest time in the 100m when I ran in my heat. The teachers said I broke the record for our school. The bad news is that Eddy got an even better time than mine in his heat. When we raced each other later in the final I couldn't keep up to him at the start. But I ran my fastest and made sure he didn't get any farther ahead of me.

I did set a record for the most 2nd place ribbons in one year. Big deal. Mom says I should be happy about being this good. She doesn't get why I want to win. I feel ripped off because I practiced this year and still lost.

June 3, 1984

Today is my 11th birthday. I got a new motorcross bike. Not really with a motor, but it has cool shocks for when I ride over bumps and jumps. I really like my bike and I rode it for a whole hour tonight during my party with friends. Mom made me a chocolate cake and we roasted hot dogs for the supper part.

Mom was actually crying when she saw how happy I was to get my bike. I don't know why she did that. I asked and she told me they were happy tears. That doesn't make sense to me. It must be because I am a boy, not a girl.

Eddy was one of the friends I invited over for my party. Mom made me invite no more than 4 boys. She said I could invite more friends if some of them were girls. Gross! Why would I do that? Anyway, Eddy didn't seem to want to go home when the party was over. I finally asked him why he didn't want to leave because it was bed time. He said he misses his Dad, and his mom makes him do jobs around the house that his Dad used to do. He said that he hoped he could just go straight to bed when he got home.

I do feel sad for Eddy. His Mom works as a waitress at the truck stop diner. She always gets home late. She's so tired that she needs Eddy to take care of his three younger sisters almost every night. Eddy says they scream a lot and only want to play with dolls all the time. I am glad I have brothers.

At school I learned that when I make a new paragraph I am supposed to make an indent thing. My teacher says that was the only thing wrong with my essay that I wrote about why Rubik's Cube was hard for me to solve.

July 4, 1984

Today was really fun for me. The weather outside was very good for riding around on my bike. Eddy has a new bike too. He got one from his Dad. We rode to the river and went wading to cool off. The fireworks tonight were totally awesome too.

Part of my day wasn't the greatest though. Other kids came to the river too while Eddy and I was there. They are the kids at school who think they are better than everyone else. When they saw the bikes that Eddy and I rode, they teased us because what we thought were new bikes, were both old ones that were fixed up, and made to look new.

Eddy and I decided today that we will always stay friends because we promised to never tease each other, even if our parents can't get us the newest stuff. I don't know why other kids have to be such jerks, but at least Eddy and I have each other.

Chapter 3: 1988

Chapter 3: 1988

September 8, 1988

    I am starting a journal project again for my English class. My teacher is Mr. Hardy, and he says writing more often may help my overall outlook toward school and life. He promised me not to read this too closely as long as it looks like I am taking it seriously. He will give me full points for it if I get 1000 words per week.

    I think he feels sorry for me since everyone knows about my mom dying over the summer. Writing might help me to feel better someday, but right now, I just feel lost. Dad is taking this very hard and he stays at work late too often. I think he might not really be working, but that's what he always says he is doing. Tomorrow I will write about mom's funeral because I have too much math homework to do.

September 9, 1988

    When Mom died I was out of town visiting at my cousin's place. Dad called me on the phone at 1:00 in the morning because it took a long time for the police to figure out how to notify the family, since the car Mom was driving was wrecked so badly. They never did find the license plate, so they had to find her driver's license to identify her. It was so hard to hear the news. I had never heard Dad's voice quiver that way. It was hard to have to hear this news over the phone, but Dad didn't want anyone else to have to tell me. The only comfort we got was the police and ambulance people figured she died instantly, so she didn't suffer.

    Three days later, we had the funeral. Mom's sister Connie shared the eulogy. I actually learned a few things about my Mom that I didn't know about her youth. She had been an excellent dancer, and considered doing that professionally before she met my Dad. If she hadn't married him, she may have become very famous. I suppose that's why she liked the arts so much. She wanted me to do music. Maybe she figured dance would be too sissy for me because I was a boy, so she pushed music lessons on me instead.

    It was nice to see all of my cousins that I don't see often enough. However, the reason for the family being together was not a reason I liked at all. I noticed that at first everyone in the family, and all our friends tried hard to be there for us. People brought meals to the house quite often that first month. After that, the concern seemed to wear off, and we were left feeling quite alone. That's when the loss of Mom really hit me hard.

September 10, 1988

Dad took us to a restaurant for dinner last night. I ran out of time to write in my journal. This is hard to talk about, but I have not cried since mom died. Dad did though. It was the first time I ever saw him do that, and it really scared me. He held on to her coffin and wanted everyone to leave the cemetery for a few minutes until he finally left. The only good thing that has happened now is that dad talks to me more because mom is not here. It's still weird though because I could talk to Mom for longer times. I will have to get used to this because I think Dad needs me.

Last year when Grandpa Palmer and Grandma Workman both died so close to the same time, it was hard enough. It was the first time I had ever been to a funeral in my life. Dad managed to not cry in front of any of us at his Mom's funeral, but I knew he did privately later on.

It makes me so sad to think of all of the people I have lost in the last 18 months. I hope that what I have learned about from Indian culture is true. I have a feeling inside that they all live somewhere. They have a spirit that lives on, and not just because I remember them. Other people might laugh at me when I talk about this stuff, but even though I miss my Mom, my Grandpa, and my Grandma, I always feel like they are watching me. It's not the way I want it, but at least they are still close to me.

Eddy and I are both going to be watching from the bench this year since we are just in 10th grade on the football team. Eddy's dad remarried and lives closer to him, so he gets to see him every week now. Eddy enjoys that, even though his dad drinks so much.

September 11, 1988

My English teacher told me to go ahead and write the good things I remember about the people I have lost. I didn't want to at first. The more I thought about, the more I realized that I love them all so much, that I wanted to remember them forever. Writing about them keeps them alive to me.

My Mother's voice is the sweetest voice I have ever heard. Sometimes a teenage boy doesn't want to do what he's told.

Chapter 3: 1988

Sometimes a boy thinks he knows more than his Mom. In my life, Mom was right more often than I admitted. What was so great about her was that she wouldn't ever say, "I told you so", no matter what happened. She never said that to Dad either. Even when she was mad at us, she found a way to tell us what she needed to without hurting anyone.

Mom never said an unkind thing about other people outside of our family either. She always tried to see the good in everyone. Whether I was doing music or sports, she was the best at cheering, and helped me to feel like I could do anything I wanted to do. She said she loved me almost every day.

September 12, 1988

I was too sad to write about everyone in one day, so I waited till tonight to finish.

Grandma Workman's cooking was very good. I have never tasted a better cream puff or gingerbread cookie in my life than when I was at her house. She tried to get me to eat vegetables too, but I never learned to like them a much as she did.

She was so patient. When we were little we would go to her house and she would help us put puzzles together. Some of them were 500 or 1000 pieces, and they take a lot of time. She taught my brothers and me the strategy for putting the pieces in piles of similar colors. Then we would put the edge pieces all together first so we could see how big the whole thing would be when it was done.

She didn't talk much about the depressing times in the 1930s, but Dad says she got very good at taking care of things when the family had so little. She lived by a saying "Do the best you can, with what you have, today."

I think she told all of us grandkids that we were her favorite. It didn't hurt my feelings when I figured that out. When I think of her now, I know that she had a big heart, and truly loved everyone in her life as much as she could. She would do anything to help someone.

My Grandpa Palmer had a great sense of humor. I didn't get to know him as well as I wanted to though. He was tired all the time, and I mostly just remember seeing him lying on his couch when we visited him. He would pull faces, tell funny stories, and sing songs that were hilarious.

Mom said he was known for being a real sports guy when he

was younger. He coached many successful baseball and basketball teams. One day I remember him telling me that he thought football was too rough, so he stayed away from it. I think equipment is better now than when he was a kid, so it's safer.

September 18, 1988

I am tied with Eddy for the most special team tackles. At least we get to play in that part of the games. I am not as fast as him really, because I am not as strong and the equipment makes me slower. I have to predict a lot to make sure I go the right places. So far that strategy is working.

Our school band is going to tour in Miami this year, as long as I can make the $150 to go. Dad says his new job at the car dealership is not going to pay much the first few months, so I need to get a job at the gas station to pay for my trip. Minimum wage is $3.50/hr here so that's pretty good. I have to work around 50 hours to save the money up.

I have noticed that no one cares about people in the band like they do about guys on the football and basketball team. I guess it is good for me to be on football then.

October 4, 1988

I didn't get all 1000 words for my journal assignment in September. It's not a good excuse but dad leaves me and the other 2 boys home a lot by ourselves. He says being 15 is an adult in some cultures, so I should be fine. I am just glad that Jared is finally potty trained. His diapers reeked. Alex is always butting in to conversations when I have friends over, or when I talk on the phone.

Sometimes I wish cassette tapes weren't invented. I would rather use records again because you can't pull the tape out and wreck them. Alex is really good at taking my cassettes, and wrapping the tape around bedposts and stuff. I did get my Def Leppard tape put back inside, but now it sounds funny when I play it. Someday I hope someone invents something better than this, or we could go back to records again. Were they really that bad?

Actually, I do know the answer to that question. It would have been pointless to invent the Sony Walkman for jogging with my own portable music player if the parts inside it were playing records,

Chapter 3: 1988

not tapes. Maybe someone will invent music out of the sound that a record makes when it skips, goes forward and backward crazily.

October 8, 1988

    I can't breathe. Today the hottest girl I ever met in real life just moved in to our town, and she is in most of my classes at school. Her name is Hope. I don't know her last name, but her skin is flawless and her eyes could melt an igloo in seconds. I hope she didn't notice me staring at her today. All the other guys at school seem to have noticed her too, so she probably didn't even notice me staring at her. I have way more homework tonight because I couldn't concentrate in class. Hope seems to be really smart too, and not afraid to talk in new situations. I don't know if I will ever get the nerve to ask her out.

October 31, 1988

    I took my little brothers out Halloweening (Is that really a word?) Anyway, they both went as ghosts and couldn't see very well. They also kept tripping because their feet kept getting tangled in the sheets they were wearing. The sheets were too big for them I think. They got wayyy--- more candy than they needed, so Dad says they have to share with me for being nice enough to take them like Mom used to. It's funny, but I think I missed Mom today more than I have for a while.

    I got my first report card today. Other than my recent troubles concentrating because of Hope, my grades were still pretty good. In Social, I am still #3 in class. In Math and Science, I am #2 behind somebody. PE I am #2 behind Eddy, but coach says my effort almost made me #1. In band, I don't know where I fit because the teacher, Mr. Simon, likes us to only know our own scores, and I don't feel like asking everyone else what they got. So, I got 92% but have no idea what that means.

    While I went with my brothers, Dad was out a really long time. I don't know where he went because he just said it was nothing he wanted me to worry about. That's kind of funny because whenever my Dad says that, I worry a little bit more each time. I think he must have a girlfriend he doesn't want me to know about yet. It would be fine to tell me. I know he must be lonely without Mom. It's the sneaky way he is doing this that bothers me.

2nd Place

December 20, 1988

Well, I was right about Dad. He has a girlfriend. She has 2 kids of her own that are much younger than me. I guess she is kind of pretty. Not someone I would have wanted to be with, but I am not 37, so that's probably why. As for my love life, funny, I don't really have one unless daydreaming counts. Hope gets better looking every day, but I have heard from other guys that she is not looking for a guy at her own school. She likes someone from another town or something. Typical.

Eddy seems to be unhappy this Christmas. His dad doesn't phone as often, and sends less money to the family. He has a new family to worry about Eddy says. At least I still have my Dad.

December 25, 1988

I think this is the first Christmas that I didn't enjoy. I got nice gifts, but seeing an empty spot at the dinner table, and not eating as well as I used to each Christmas was so hard for me. I didn't feel like eating at dinnertime. After seeing Mom's empty stocking hanging above the fireplace, I couldn't stand it anymore. I went to my room, and finally cried about Mom dying.

Alex and Jared tried to come into my room to comfort me, but I kicked them out. Nothing and nobody will ever replace Mom. Dad rescued me, and got the boys to leave me alone. Then he made them play with their new toys downstairs so he could talk to me alone.

I don't remember much about what he said, but I do remember how much better I felt after. Dad seems to have a magical way of talking me through things that are hard.

Chapter 4: 1989

Chapter 4: 1989

April 4, 1989

Our band trip to Miami was so much fun. I managed to save enough money from my job to pay for the whole thing myself. I didn't realize just how pretty a place Miami is. Miami Vice showed some of it, but focused more on the bad guys, weird clothes, and stuff like that. Seeing something on TV is so different from seeing it in person.

Our teacher, Mr. Simon, had us very well prepared to perform at festivals. We had some excellent ratings, and the adjudicators really liked the attention to detail we showed in our performances.

Mr. Simon is so fun and energetic, and that keeps us all interested in his class. I have been in his class for so many years, and it is much different than when I took piano lessons when I was little. For some reason it doesn't bother me like other musical activities. I miss Mom so much, and music usually reminds me of her.

April 14, 1989

I tried out for the track team today. I am a little out of shape still because the only other sport I play is football, and that ended last November. Coach Sloan says I have the drive but need the engine tuned up. I don't get what he means yet. Eddy of course is on the team too. He doesn't even have to try. I am quite jealous of that. He doesn't even work out, and his biceps get the girls to flock around him like vultures around some road kill. It's not fair. I work way harder on things than he does, and he still comes out ahead. I am still Eddy's friend, but he is starting to annoy me.

June 3, 1989

It happened today. Dad married Jennifer. He thought it was going to be a bit of a surprise. He waited until Easter to tell us boys, and us older two laughed because we already saw him kissing her at the movies one time. He didn't know we had come to see the show too. Everybody and their dog wanted to see Twins with Danny DeVito and Arnold Schwarzennenger Schwarzenegger. I'm sure both tries on that name were wrong, but whoever reads this later will probably know who that guy is, he has been in lots of movies.

The wedding was okay I guess. My littlest brother Jared got to be the ring boy, or whatever they call that. The ceremony would have been perfect except that Jared sneezed all over the wedding ring just before handing it to the preacher guy. Alex started laughing, and so did Jennifer. I think we will like Jennifer just fine, but I don't think I can ever call her Mom. It just doesn't seem to fit.

September 4, 1989

I will be a starter on the football team this year. I'll play receiver on offence, and will get some duty as defensive back as well. Coach Walker says it depends on my conditioning.

I like coach Walker. He is determined to win every game. He is intense with us, tells us when we've done right or wrong, just so there is no doubt about our performance on the field. Ace is our quarterback this year, and he can sure throw the ball. Coach Walker says this is the best team he's ever coached, and we have our best shot ever to win the state championship.

Eddy, of course, is a starter too. There are enough spots on the team that I don't think I will have to compete with him for playing time. That's great news.

September 5, 1989

It's funny but now that journal writing isn't an assignment for my English class, I enjoy doing this more, and I may end up writing more this year than I did last year. If it's my idea first, I can get used to doing pretty much anything.

I looked at some old photos of our family the other day. I still can't believe Mom is not here anymore. I know she'd want me to write more about musical stuff, so I will mention some of that here again. I signed up for band class again, but this year, I am also with the jazz group that practices after school. Mr. Simon sure seems to love this kind of music. I wasn't really into it at first, but after hearing a few recordings he played for us on the old record player, I am suddenly much more interested. So far, I like Duke Ellington's music the best of all.

My instrument in band class is the clarinet, but in jazz I get to play the piano. Mr. Simon says someone who plays by ear like me could use a challenge like this. The sheet music he gives me to play often doesn't have much to look at, other than chord symbols. Once in awhile a riff will be written out fully in regular notes. I guess it's ok with me, now that I am interested in learning the names of the

Chapter 4: 1989

chords I've been messing around with, before I knew what they were called.

September 12, 1989

We are starting to see that we are as good a team as Coach Walker thinks we are. We are undefeated so far this year. But coach keeps telling us that we haven't beaten anyone good yet. Next weekend we play against our biggest rivals – the Lions. They are undefeated too. Should be a good game, and we get to be the home team.

September 18, 1989

Tonight we played the Lions. I really don't like them. I found their defensive players to be quite dirty. They jabbed me in the throat at the line of scrimmage, if the ref had his back turned. They reach under the facemask and try to scratch a guy's face. Since the facemask doesn't get jerked or bumped, the refs don't seem to catch this stuff.

Eddy even said they were holding him at the line because they had heard about his great speed. We were expected to have a close game with them, but after all the clutching, grabbing and cheating, they thumped us 45-7. Eddy got our only touchdown on a kickoff return.

The Lion's quarterback is a guy named Ralph Jones. Well, he goes by the name Derrick, but I heard his first name is actually Ralph and he hates it, so I will always make a point of calling him Ralph. This jerk also plays defensive back. Once in awhile, he played head-to-head against me. What a talker. I have never heard so much whining, spouting off, or rudeness in my life. If that's what it takes to be successful, it makes me wonder if it's worth it. I think the way I play should speak for itself.

Anyway, Ralph found out about my Mom dying, and called me a 'momma's boy with no momma'. What a complete moron this guy is. I hope someone smacks him hard this year. That probably won't happen because his team has a tough offensive line to protect him.

September 29, 1989

Eddy was injured in practice this week. Coach Walker says they will pass the ball to me a little more because he's not playing in the game next weekend. We only have one loss this year, so the season is going well.

Hope was watching the practice when Eddy got hurt. It seemed to me that she was way too sympathetic. She must have liked him from a distance for a while. When he went down hard and then grabbed his foot in pain, she was one of the first people out on the field to see if he was OK. It was just an ankle sprain, but Eddy seemed to milk it for all it was worth. Ever since she helped him off the field, they started hanging around together. What do I have to do to get her attention?

I did have some fun at practice this week. Playing jokes on people is so much fun. I pretended I couldn't remember my lock combination, so I asked if I could borrow the master key during my gym class this morning. I still had the key during lunch, so I waited until no one was around during noon hour. I went and put some deep heat lotion on the jock straps of most of the rookies on our team. They all have to use the junky looking lockers at the far end of the change room, so it is easy to make sure I only got rookies. I gave the key back right before lunch ended.

To cover the smell of the deep heat, I made a point of being early to the change room, and pretended to need some deep heat lotion on my calf muscles. I had Eddy apply it, and then a couple of other players figured they needed some too. No one suspected a thing when they got dressed.

Practice started as usual after we all got suited up. The young guys seemed to have no idea anything was wrong until we started doing our warm-up sprints. Then, one at a time they started dancing around like their butts were on fire. I acted alone, and will never tell anyone! Rookies are so fun to tease.

October 4, 1989

We had a great game last weekend. I scored 2 touchdowns, got to play on kickoff returns, had the most yardage for every offensive category. We beat City Central High School. They have a big, slow team and have only won 2 games all year. Even though it was an easier opponent, it still felt good to do well and show what I can do too. I think I am just as valuable to the team as Eddy is.

Hope and Eddy watched the game from the sideline. She seems to really like him. My performance on the field didn't get her attention

Chapter 4: 1989

at all. I'm fine. There are girls at my school who seem to like me, and they flirt a little. I guess the attention is fun, but I have always liked Hope since the first day I saw her at school. I always wish she would tease me.

October 31, 1989

I love Halloween. Now that my brothers are old enough to trick-or-treat by themselves, I went out to raise a little hell. (I like the song too!) Mostly, Eddy and I just did toilet paper and stuff like that. But, after midnight a fog rolled in, just like in a freaky movie. That was perfect. Eddy and I could sneak around better and not be detected.

We went to Mr. Smith's house. He's our school principal. I waxed every window on his car. As a total gag, I actually spelled my own name on it. No idiot would ever write his own name, so I will get out of this one I am sure.

November 2, 1989

The police came by my house and asked me to go with them to Mr. Smith's house. I told them Eddy and I had done toilet papering only, and that only an idiot would write their own name on a car they were waxing. They let me off for lack of evidence. Mr. Smith just sort of smiled while I left. I think I was pretty convincing.

November 7, 1989

Last Friday was our first playoff game of this season. We won quite easily against Central High School. The final score was not really a good description of how it went. By the end of the 3rd quarter, we were winning 45-0. We had our subs in during the 4th quarter, and the final score was 52-17. Eddy had 3 touchdowns, and I had 2. Eddy had 2 interceptions on defense, and I had a fumble recovery.

This weekend, we played a bigger, faster team, the Rams. They were tougher to play, but we still won 21-10. Eddy got all 3 touchdowns, but I had more yards than him. Coach Walker seems to be showcasing Eddy with the play calling when we are in scoring range. I heard there were some college scouts at our game. Our next game is actually for the State Championship, and we have to play the Lions again, the only team we lost to this year.

2nd Place

November 14, 1989

I am so disappointed with our last game. We had the Lions down by 7 points with 10 minutes left to go. We should have won. Ralph Jones was his normal cheating and loud-mouthed self. I could just clobber him for what he says and does. Anyway, he managed to get the tying touchdown himself with a little trick play that was going to be a field goal. I admit he is good at faking handoffs and stuff like that. He's lucky I was not playing on defence for that play. I would have nailed him.

We had a chance to take the lead again, but I dropped a pass at the 5-yard line that was thrown way behind me. I only got one hand on it. Our last play before time ran out in the fourth quarter would have been a field goal for the win if I had caught the long pass before that. We ended up going to overtime. We couldn't score on our 3 possessions, and the Lions got a field goal and 2 touchdowns. The final score was 37-20. Makes it sound like we got slaughtered, but it was closer than that before overtime.

Coach Walker tried to be nice to us during his speech after the game, but I can tell he is really disappointed in out efforts toward the end. I guess it was more mental mistakes. We weren't our best because we were all so tired by then. The hometown crowd seemed to help the Lions take the momentum away for good.

Looking back on our season, there were so many good times. We had games where we came together as a team, fought back to retake the lead in the end, stuff like that. To have our season end this way seems unfair in a way because it puts a big black cloud over something that was quite bright before that. I also find that I am getting tired of finishing 2nd all the time. I work harder at things than most people my age. I don't understand why I can't be the best at something. I do believe in God, but I sometimes wonder if he is punishing me for something because he never lets me win it all.

Life isn't all bad. Dad was at every one of my games this year. Since he married Jennifer, I have noticed that he is a lot more relaxed. He does still like to take her on dates and leave me at home with the boys too much, but I can tell he is making an effort to be a bigger part of my life at the same time. It seems to be Jennifer's idea that he does this for me. She will never replace my mother, but I do respect her. She is easygoing, fun, and it surprises me how much she knows about football. Not bad for a girl. Ha Ha!

Chapter 4: 1989

She says she was one of the first girls to play powder-puff football when she was in high school. I wouldn't want to see her play now, but I wouldn't mind seeing Hope in a football uniform. Oh Baby! Who am I kidding? She likes Eddy. I guess other girls would look good in a football uniform too. No one else seems to have it all like Hope, so I guess I will just have to be a Hopeless romantic. (Yes, the pun is intended, dang those English class lessons.)

November 22, 1989

I have still been losing sleep over our lost game to the Lions. I am so depressed that we didn't win that one. It hurts to be that close to victory, only to have it slip away. Maybe it would be easier to take if it had been anyone else but Ralph Jones. He is such an in-your-face jerk about things. I pity anyone who marries this punk, or has anything to do with him later on in life. What comes around goes around, and I'd like to see him get his just reward.

Chapter 5: 1990

Chapter 5: 1990

February 14, 1990

It was our school's Valentine's Dance tonight. Traditionally, this event is girl's choice. One of our cheerleaders named Diane asked me to it. She's great actually. Pretty, fun, says whatever she is thinking. I had previously been a guy who didn't kiss on the first date, but she made me change my mind. I may have to ask her out again sometime. An evening with Diane is quite an adventure.

May 1, 1990

Last weekend was our Senior Prom. I don't graduate this year, but my plan was to take Diane to the dance, and have a good time. That all happened just fine, mostly. The REAL story happens way before that.

I was dressed up and ready to go, had the flowers ready, some chocolate gift-wrapped. I felt like I was totally prepared for the big night. Dad gave me a car last month, and I have really loved having some wheels that are mine. The night before, I spent hours shining it up. When I got out the back door to head over to Diane's, I couldn't believe my eyes. Someone had taken all four wheels off, laid them flat on the ground, and rested the car up on the wheels.

Well, I was quite ticked off by this. I grabbed Dad's jack from the shed, and got pretty dirty fixing things back up. I went back inside and tried to clean up as best as I could. I was now 30 minutes late for everything. Dad wasn't around tonight. He and Jennifer were on a date somewhere.

When I got in the driver's seat finally, there was a note taped to the steering wheel. All it said was. "Only an idiot would put his name on a car he had pranked – D.S." I thought about this for a while. Who the heck was D.S. I wondered? I didn't have any friends or enemies at school with those initials.

I got to the dance with Diane, and was wandering around awhile, still feeling pretty sheepish for being so late for it. I happened to hear someone walk by the principal and say, "Great graduation speech Doug." Then it hit me. Doug Smith was D. S. I looked back him. He gave me that smile; just like he had the night I convinced the cops I was no idiot.

I guess he paid me back, but really, what he did to me took much less work to fix back. When I waxed his windows, I knew it was going to be pretty hard to get off afterward. Maybe I am not quite a man yet, but I am a changed man now. I think my pranking is behind me.

Oh, I almost forgot to mention the dance itself. The decorations were kind of odd. I couldn't tell if we were trapped in a science fiction movie set, or if someone had just made a mess with paper, and then just glued it to the walls. Does pink even go with green, or was it teal? Why do girls have to see the world with so many specific colors anyway? I am lucky to remember all six colors of the spectrum in science classes.

Diane had helped make the decorations, so my opinion of them was quickly silenced. She told me to just shut up and dance. We'd arrived late, and I had mocked her streamers, so I had no right to be a jerk the rest of the evening. I guess she was right. I was very quiet the rest of the night, but danced like crazy. Have to say, I can do a pretty good moonwalk and worm.

When the evening was over, I did apologize to Diane for everything that had gone wrong. You know, she was a pretty good sport. I think I gave myself a worse time over everything than she did.

I came home a little earlier than I thought I was going to. I was pretty tired, partly from the stress of fixing my tire problem in such a rush. When I got home, Dad and Jennifer were watching television together in the living room. I reported on most of my evening, and then I asked how theirs had been, and things all seemed pretty normal. I was just about to head to bed, and then Dad asked me how D.S. was doing.

I asked how he knew who D.S. was. He let me know that Mr. Smith had talked to him soon after the Halloween prank, and mentioned that he had actually seen me do it. I asked how that was possible, and the answer was pretty funny. Mr. Smith had frightened some kids too much with his spooky sounds, and upset his wife. They got into a bit of an argument, and he had gone for a drive to cool down, and figure out how to apologize to her.

When he got home, he felt pretty bad, but wasn't ready to go inside yet. He leaned the seat back and was considering sleeping for a bit. The windows fogged up slightly, to the point that Eddy and I had no idea he was in the car. Silly me, I forgot that Dad and Mr. Smith were friends in high school. He and my Dad had agreed to wait awhile and get even at a time I least suspected it. I wasn't actually going to get a car this soon, but Dad felt this would be the best way to teach me a lesson.

Chapter 6: 1991-1992

Chapter 6: 1991-1992

September 14, 1991

Wow, I can't believe I went this long without writing in this journal. I promised mom on the day of her funeral that I would write more, though I couldn't see her. I know that somehow she knew what I was saying though. It was like she was there, but not. I think there is a God, and I hope he is treating her well until she sees me again.

My brothers say they miss having me around. Dad and Jennifer still go out a lot, and leave the kids at home too much. At least I think it is too much. Jared says I was a better babysitter than Alex. Now it's their turn to see what it's like taking care of a household of kids almost every weekend. My turn is over, and I really like life here at university. I am so far from home. My Chevy SS Nova is still running, although I don't know if it will get me back home now. Funny smell if I leave it idling too long.

I can't believe that Eddy managed to get a high enough score on the entrance tests to qualify for university. I think it had more to do with the fact that he was the fastest kid in the 100m and 200m in our state track meet. As usual, I was a close second, but didn't have a fast enough time to qualify for a track scholarship. Eddy still calls me for help with his homework. This is really bothering me that he has an athletic scholarship to be here, but I'm the one helping him to just survive his exams. I will get over it. At least Eddy isn't a jerk about beating me in races. He could be jerk if he wanted to.

There are many cute girls here at university, but no one really stands out, well, not yet anyway. Hope is here too, no surprise there, but she likes Eddy. Yeah, I hate that. I've had the biggest crush on her for years, and she likes a guy who can't even read a geography textbook without a tour guide. Where is the justice in this world? I guess I am happy overall, but life could be better still. I'll see when I have time to write again.

December 17, 1991

Wow this test week was very intense. I think I got most of the questions right on my Statistics and Probability final. Music classes were a joke, but I don't mind getting really high marks to boost the GPA. I love watching basketball and football games here. What a change from back home with maybe 50 people watching.

I talked to the track coach, Bob Harris. Based on my times in the

100m and 200m at state finals when I lost to Eddy, I may still have a shot at making the team. I would REALLY like to be on the team, so I have started training. I am doing two workouts per day for now. My weight is a little too high for a sprinter, but I can get that down by playing hoops I am sure.

January 14, 1992

I went to a movie tonight with Desiree. She plays clarinet in the band I am in as my extra-curricular class. We had a great time. I think the movie was called 'Big', but I didn't see much of it, we were sitting too close together. In case my kids ever read this, I am speaking in code here to prevent you from being embarrassed.

Desiree is really great for me. Other girls I have gone out with are so uptight all the time and don't know how to relax or just talk about normal stuff. She is not athletic, but she cheers me on, so that's fine. She thinks that I have more depth to my personality. She likes that I love sports and winning so much, but that I also have talent in music and art too. She thinks I will make the track team here, and I hope she is right. In my experience, it matters more to others if I am good at sports.

No one cares that I am musical. That's also why I have declared myself a PE major instead of Music. I will teach gym someday, unless I make the big time and somehow can break into professional sports first. There are walk-on spots available here on the football team, and I think after succeeding in track this spring, I will have some good luck afterward.

April 2, 1992

I am on the track team, but I have to wait until next year to compete. Eddy won 3rd at the NCAA finals this year. My overall GPA after one year at university was 3.82. Eddy got 2.56, which is just barely high enough to keep his track scholarship. He at least was nice enough to take me to dinner to thank me for all of my help this year.

Desiree and I are just going to be friends. We couldn't see marriage being a real option, as some day I either want to be playing pro football, or teaching PE back home. All of her family lives here, and she doesn't want to leave. It's heart breaking because we had something special, but I think we would regret it later not being able to live near other people we want to be close to.

Even though I understand why we won't be together, it is still hard to let go of Desiree. I was so depressed about our breakup that I wrote a song about this. The words are as follows:

I was going through the motions
Figured life was fine
Then I knew something was missing
I'll always cherish the time

CHORUS:
Sweet was the joy when I met you Baby
I found some meaning for life
I'm getting better at trusting my heart
But I'm not very good at good-bye

We're not that different from others around us
We all get sad sometimes
What we've got is worth the struggle
Just take my hand, we'll be fine

CHORUS

When I'm with you, time just flies
Can't seem to get enough
This aint some poor fool's addiction
I'd like to call it love

CHORUS

The song is just with two guitar parts, nothing else. I recorded it at a friend's place with his Fostex 8-track recorder. That part of the project was fun to do.

The writing was a bit too painful. I know the words make it sound like things aren't over. The indecision is making it too painful to completely let go. I am left wondering why I always seem to fall for what can't be. It always seems like everyone else finds that special someone, and he or she lives happily ever after. When is it my turn?

Chapter 7: 1993

March 3, 1993

Man the course load was tougher this year. They really seem to want to kill us with the workload as Education students. I have not been as good with my training, but I got my weight down, and my times in my events are better than any other point in my life. I feel healthy and energetic, but a little worn down. The national finals are next week, and I think both Eddy and I have a good shot for a medal. That's saying a lot since we are only second year men racing against seniors.

Hope knows I like her. Eddy let it slip one day, and she has been teasing me ever since. I hate that. She says she'll date the one of us who wins or at least has a better showing at the finals. I have not felt so motivated about a race my entire life. Some NFL scouts are supposed to be there too, as I hear some teams are trying to find some faster players to help with the west coast offence teams are using these days. I would LOVE to play pro football before my teaching career. That would be so great to have some fun first before having to be serious all the time.

March 5, 1993

I am so prepared for the finals on the 10th. In training today, I had a personal best time, and was actually stride for stride with Eddy in one of our practice runs. I can't remember a time in my life when my body felt more powerful, flexible, and yet durable. I have been eating right this year, and my weight is perfect for sprinting.

Another great thing I have been doing is yoga and some deep breathing techniques. I never thought this stuff would help my running so much. Getting oxygen to the muscles more efficiently is such a rush. I can tell it is making me faster. It is so cool to know that I couldn't possibly be any faster than I am right now. I was only .01 seconds slower than Eddy today, and that's not saying much because we didn't have the most accurate timers today. I may have actually beaten him in the run I did without him. 1st place is in my grasp, and I just need to run the race of my life next week.

March 10, 1993

This will go down as the most memorable day of my life so far, but for all the wrong reasons. It started fine. Eddy and I had personal best times yesterday. We had eaten at just the right times. The track was good, the weather was calm, it was sunny, but not too hot. Eddy and I were both pumped but not too hyper.

Eddy won the 200, and I got 3rd. The 100m race is my real event, so I hoped to do better in that one. We both sailed through the heats, with each of us winning the one we ran. In the final, I had the inside lane, but Eddy just had too much for me in last 50 metres.

In the 100m heats, Eddy was 1st in his, and I was 2nd in mine, but my time was in the top 4. As the day wore on, I couldn't help but think back to all the times Eddy and have raced each other in the last few years. It was pretty great to have Eddy and I both in the final.

When the 100m final actually happened, we had one false start from some guy from out east. I noticed as I got in the starting position again, that we had a slight head wind, but I remained focused and didn't let anything bother me.

When we finally got going, I had my best start ever. I could see daylight on both sides of my peripheral vision, so I knew I had the early lead. I was breathing perfectly, the strides were flowing nicely, I felt no tension anywhere, and my muscles were all doing their job. I still felt like I had one more gear to shift into, and I did. I loved the way the breeze felt on my face as I thrust through it.

Halfway through the race I could hear the crowd starting to roar, as someone must have been catching up for a close finish. There was no one on my right that I could see, that was Eddy's side, but I could tell someone on my left was gaining.

I didn't turn to look. I fought off the urge to do that. I tried to lengthen my strides just a little and maintain my striding pace, but suddenly two strides before the finish, there was Eddy passing me for 1st place. I was second by 0.25 seconds. I was happy to have a medal to show for it, but for once in my life, I just wanted to beat him. The 100m is over all too quickly some times. I knew I had a personal best time, even before going to the scorer's table.

What happened next was about as demoralizing a thing as I have ever witnessed. Eddy was surrounded immediately by a hoard of NFL scouts, asking if he'd consider quitting university and playing football now. The guy from out east who got 3rd was later approached over me because I heard one scout say he was impressed with his acceleration after his poor start, as he had been spooked by his false start from before.

Not one of them talked to me. It was hard to hide my

disappointment. I couldn't make the scouts talk to me, and I didn't think approaching them was my place either. A silver medal seemed like it may have been enough to get their attention, but it's obviously not.

As the crowds and athletes left, I stayed behind and looked at the track, replaying the race in my mind over and over. I honestly can't think of anything I could have done differently. My preparation was fine, and the best ever for me. I work harder than most of the people who competed at the track today. It hurt deeply to be completely ignored this way. I still think I will race next year. Eddy says he is tempted to go to the NFL now, and not finish school.

As for me, I would not quit school now, but I would like to play football afterward. I may not ever get the chance. Would it upset something in the universe if I were to actually win something?

May 25, 1993

I have chosen to stay here and take summer school. Not because I had any poor grades, just because I want to finish school sooner. I can't believe how much life has changed in just over a month. Eddy has signed with the Cleveland Browns. He is on the practice roster for sure, but they have promised him some bonus money if he really turns heads in training camp. He may make the top roster and see some action in the pre-season. He informs me that he is quitting school completely to pursue his dream of the NFL. He says he'll make enough to retire on, and hire people to run his finances so he is okay as an old man later.

I wish I were the one in the NFL instead. I would save the money wisely, and still probably teach afterward just because I think I would like the job. Eddy doesn't phone as much these days. The physical demands of training drain him. He only seems to have time for Hope and football. Somehow I knew she was never going to think of me the way she thinks of him. I'll be fine somehow.

September 4, 1993

I have at least found a girl who I think is even better suited to me than I thought Hope was. Her name is Kerry.

Kerry and I met in my Education Foundations class. She will be doing Early Childhood Education. It is a lucky break for me that she even needed a class I am in, since we are not planning to teach the same age group. Anyway, look at me getting so serious this soon. I have known Kerry for only a week, but there is some chemistry there I just can't ignore.

When I first met Kerry, she was already in class, and I was arriving 30-45 seconds late. She noticed me looking around with a, "Where the heck am I going to sit?" look on my face. She sort of waved, and pointed to the seat next to her. From where I was, I didn't realize there was one more seat there. I thanked her for being so kind to me. Then I warned her to be cautious around strangers. I think she liked that I tried to be funny. I was trying very hard to listen to the instructor, but I kept catching myself looking at her hair. She sure smelled good too.

Tonight, there was a dance on campus. It was a Hawaiian Beach Theme. Kerry was actually one of the people in charge of it. I didn't know that ahead of time, but when she greeted me at the door, and put a white lay lei around my neck, something happened to me. Sure, there were numerous attractive girls there that night, but the more time I spent with Kerry, the deeper she pulled me in.

Talking to her didn't feel like a job interview. I had a feeling come over me that I could tell her my secrets, hopes, dreams, joys, pains, and that she would understand and talk back. It's hard to explain this about my self. I am usually more careful about how much I tell a person when I first get to know them. It's different with Kerry. I get to be me now. We like the same music, subjects at school, politicians, public speakers, and authors.

For me, it felt by the end of the evening like I had just spent it with my best friend. She offered her phone number to me. I was motionless and speechless, and finally clued in and wrote it down. I didn't want the evening to end, but it eventually had to once the cleanup was done, and I walked her home. Even the way she walks is charming. I am so completely smitten.

Eddy has really done well in Cleveland. Not only is he on the main roster and enjoying his signing bonus, but also the guy ahead of him got hurt, and he has to start the season at wide receiver. What good luck he always has.

Though it's sometimes hard for me to watch all of this, I am very happy that I have found Kerry. Would be harder if I felt all alone these days.

Chapter 7: 1993

September 27, 1993

Kerry and I were talking the other day, and her hometown is only one hour away from mine. We are quite thrilled with that. I was actually scared to ask where she was from because I figured I'd have the same result as I had with Desiree. Kerry and I both want to live near family, so we will not have to break up over this. I guess we could still find other reasons, but I just can't see any today.

I know. It's really early to even be thinking anything long term, but I am type of guy who doesn't want to waste someone else's time if it's not going to work out. Kerry has a way of talking that draws me in.

I have never known anyone so smart, yet still speaks to me like an equal. Some girls try to impress so much that it chases a guy away. My favorite part about Kerry is still her hair. Some styles these days have girls with really short hair, and it doesn't strike me as feminine. I like longer hair on a woman. Call me old-fashioned. I don't care.

I actually got to watch Eddy in action on TV last weekend. Teams are not used to defending a man with his speed. He has played 3 games now, and already has 250 yards and two touchdowns. He's only a rookie, and defensive coaches are using double coverage against him. It's almost unheard of what he is able to do at such a young age.

Chapter 8: 1994

Chapter 8: 1994

January 19, 1994

Cleveland didn't make the playoffs this year, but Eddy still had a great year. There is talk he may be traded to a team that is a contender next year. We have to wait and see.

He came to visit me last weekend. He drove up in his new spiffed up Mustang. I thought he'd get something even flashier. Oh well, I guess that's a good thing. He and Hope are getting married. With their location being so up in the air, she has taken a break from university herself, and has no idea when she will resume her studies. Kind of a waste really, I thought she was pretty smart.

Kerry and I are still seeing each other quite a bit. We met each other's families at Christmas. That was a little bit nerve-wracking for me, as her Dad is a Lutheran Minister, or was it a Catholic Priest? I can't remember. Oh yeah, Catholic Priests don't marry. I think I remember now what he is.

Dad and the boys were glad I came home too. It meant that Kerry and I could babysit while he and Jennifer went out to his office New Year's Party. He has taken a new job at the town supermarket as the manager. He's actually really good at the job since he already knows his customers and employees very well. Jennifer is having a baby in August, so that will make life even more interesting for them.

Anyway, the night Kerry and I did hang out with my brothers, they teased me for having a girlfriend, tried to catch a peek of me kissing her good night before she went to sleep in the spare bedroom. Even after I finally got to bed on the couch in the living room, they were still hassling me. I guess they really missed me when I was at school.

I spoke to a career counselor at university today. I am on pace to graduate by April as planned. He claims that few people are able to do the summer school thing and finish early like this. That was welcome news. It's expensive being here. The downside is, there aren't many jobs where I want to be right now. I have to wait 2 years to apply at my hometown high school. Coach Sloan retires then, and he wants me to take his place. He has no say in the matter, but it is great to know he values me that much.

Kerry graduates this year too, and her prospects are better than mine. A junior high position is open in her hometown next year, and the principal there has already called her to see if she wants the job. It's not what you know; it's who you know. I guess that is good when things go the way you want. Kerry will have to teach outside her major for now, but she doesn't seem to mind. This is all speculation at this point though, we can't be sure she will be hired.

March 1, 1994

My career counselor called me this morning to inform me that my grades may be high enough to receive a special award. In the education department they give an award each year to the student who scores the highest in student teaching rounds. The prize is a refund on the tuition for their two most costly semesters. I am close to winning this if I can just get a slightly better score in my evaluations. The money would be nice. I am trying to figure out a way to pay for Kerry's wedding ring!

Yes, we are getting married this summer. I pulled some strings and got the basketball team to carry a banner onto the court for their last home game with the message "Marry me Kerry" on it. She was thrilled, jumped around like she'd won the lottery or something.

The whole event made me feel like a king. I have to admit I am amazed every day that she loves me. She is so smart, cute, and easy going. She could have anyone she wanted, but she chose me. We see each other as often as we can. That's hard to do with the workload we have these days.

We will be married at the church in her hometown. I guess this will make me a Lutheran now. I am fine with that. I owe God some devotion because he has blessed me with Kerry, and a good education.

April 24, 1994

It's finally over – I finished my last exam, and assuming my grades are about the same as last semester, I will have a teaching degree, and somewhere near a 3.50 GPA. I was 2nd in my education courses, so the cash award went to someone else. Ultimately, it's not a life-altering event to win that award, and it won't get me a job any faster, but I really wanted to win this. In one of my student teaching rounds, I saw a kid wearing a t-shirt that read: "2nd place is the first loser." Today, that message feels right, and it really bugs me.

Chapter 9: 1995

Chapter 9: 1995

August 17-28, 1995

I'd probably get shot if I didn't list this as the happiest time of my life, at least to this point anyway. Kerry and I got married on the 17th, and we've been in Hawaii ever since. It's so handy that we go to the same church now. (I joined hers) There have been no awkward moments, no explanations. There has only been peace and joy like a wedding should be. It is fitting that we are here in Hawaii, since the first dance we had was that dance at university with the same theme to it.

I know that for a woman, the wedding is all about the dress. For me, it was all about how perfect the day was. The weather couldn't have been better. There was no rain, just sun, not too hot though. All my siblings were able to attend, and the same for Kerry.

Other people did the decorating so Kerry could relax. She called the shots in the planning, but had her best friend Penni put the plan into action. What a great idea. Kerry was able to worry only about getting herself ready, and she slept well the night before. I don't think that happens very often. I made some great friends at school who formed a band. They specialize in weddings and office parties, so I hired them for our wedding.

The honeymoon? There are some sweet things a man shouldn't talk about. Suffice it to say it was memorable for all the right reasons.

Our favorite gift by far was our bedroom furniture, from Kerry's parents. They sure know what their daughter likes. She cried for a full minute when she saw it in our apartment just before we left for Hawaii. Her parents went to great lengths to make her think their only gift for her was a new electric piano. She liked that too. She's pretty easy to please, and that's the quality I love most about her. It doesn't hurt that she's gorgeous either!

I re-read the last few entries in here, and I have not mentioned yet that I start my dream job next month. After sub teaching and waiting tables for a year, I finally get to teach P.E. at the junior high school I attended all those years ago. To fill in the whole assignment, I will also be doing Grade 7 History and Science. Next year, Mr. McMurray from the high school is retiring, so I will most likely take on P.E. 7-12, and travel between the two schools.

The commute shouldn't be a problem, since they still share the same football field and track. I refer to it as a gopher hole paradise with a ring of dirty, weed infested shale around it. Someday, I hope we get a better field. Mr. Doug Smith (D.S.) is still the principal at the high school. I saw him the other day and assured him I am still not an idiot.

Kerry is still doing the substitute teaching thing for now, and she works as a receptionist for our one and only lawyer in town 2 days a week when his office is open. Not much happens here really, but it is a big job for one person to run that office. She wants to teach Art or Home Economics some day. In small schools, she will have to teach other subjects too to get a job.

Luckily, we have managed to find a home to buy. We have signed a rent-to-purchase agreement for now, but I think we will save enough money to buy it before the 3-year term expires. At least I hope so.

I was watching a sports update on television the other day, and noticed that Eddy is making headlines again. This time he is being traded because he demanded to go to a contender, and doesn't want to play for the New York Jets anymore. They finished with a 3-13 record last year, though I felt that he was not thrown to often enough. It remains to be seen whether he will get his wish.

I think he is foolish to sit out of training camp and pout until he gets his way. In what other profession could an employee do that and get away with it? We live in a strange world. With his good luck though, Eddy will probably end up with the Packers or the 49ers for this season. They both had winning records last year.

September 4, 1995

I hate being right sometimes. Eddy will be playing for the Packers. They have good coaching and a tough up and coming QB named Brett Favre. Maybe Eddy will have a championship there soon. I wish he would have gone to San Francisco instead, that's my favorite team. Eddy will be making more money in one year than I do in 10 years. Maybe he will pay more income tax and that will even things up.

The last time Eddy dropped by for a visit, he was driving a Mercedes Benz C Class, which was car of the year for 1994. Nice car I guess, but why green? I don't understand. He got it customized an ugly color. Maybe he knew he was headed for Green Bay ahead of time, and didn't tell me that part. All I can say about Eddy the person is that he is still pretty decent to me.

Chapter 9: 1995

His image in magazines is not as pleasant. He comes across as moody, rude, selfish, but very good at football, so everyone loves him anyway. My opinion doesn't matter much, but I hope he is as good to others as he is to me, and that it's just the media that is trying to make him look bad. If I were in his shoes, I know it would be hard to be in the spotlight all the time, and have people watch your every move, just for a story to tell. Someday those camera people are going to end up hurting someone more than they thought they would. The lengths some of them must go to are so outrageous, just for a picture that hurts a celebrity's image.

I have been asked to coach football and basketball this year, as there just aren't enough teachers or parents to cover all the extras at our school. I know I will be busy, but it's worth it to secure this job for the long term. I know football very well, but basketball will be a real challenge. I can play it fairly well, but have never coached it.

October 4, 1995

I watched the news tonight, and heard that O. J. Simpson was found not guilty of murdering his wife. I have watched this story off and on for the last few months. As a fan of football, I have always hoped he was innocent. He was a hero of mine, and I liked that he got to be in some movies too. Even though he got off, I still don't know if he is innocent. If he goes on to live a good life, I think that will show his true character.

December 25, 1995

Kerry and I are going to be parents next September! We just got the news from her doctor. Home pregnancy tests are not always that reliable, so the official word sounds better. I hope it's a boy! This news is a wonderful Christmas present in itself.

Chapter 10: 1996

Chapter 10: 1996

February 27, 1996

All but one team makes it to the playoffs in our basketball league. We won one game this year, so the team we beat missed out. We traveled to the city this afternoon to play the top seed in our division. Those city kids are so much faster, more skilled, and their coach knows more about the game. I am still just a football guy trying to learn a new trick I suppose. The game was not even close. By halftime we were down by 35 points.

All season long, I have rewarded the top assist getter on the team with a milkshake after each game. It's the only incentive I give my players. Since it was looking like this was going to be our last game this year, I wanted something positive to happen. These boys of mine have played with so much heart, and have gotten so close as friends and teammates.

I looked at our stat sheet and realized that one of my seniors who came to every practice and every game had not scored a point all season. He was the only player who hadn't yet, and I doubt he got much if any last year either. His parents had also come to every game to watch him play. At that moment, I knew we needed to get him the ball more and give him a chance. However, I also knew the opposition would be tough to score on, as they were a fast, aggressive, 'in our face' type of team.

While my boys were shooting to warm up for the second half, I approached the opposition coach, and let him know that I wanted #5, Joey, on our side to score his first ever points. I knew he wouldn't make the high school team, since there would be more competition. I explained that he could make shots in practice, but he'd probably not score in a game unless he was able to take uncontested shots. The other coach could see that it meant a lot to me to see one of my guys succeed. Since the game was already out of reach, he agreed to tell his players to let #5 shoot from wherever he got the ball.

Without telling my team I had talked with the opposition coach, I announced that whoever gave Joey the ball to assist on his first points of the year was going to win the milkshake for tonight. I also told them that they were only allowed to score themselves if they rebounded one of his shots first. Joey went back and shot a few more times to prepare. I think he missed them all.

The second half started quite differently than the first half had. My boys were on a mission for Joey, and they played so much more assertively. They fought harder for the ball than they had all season, just for a chance to pass it Joey. They also out rebounded the other team during the second half, which was tremendous, considering our size and speed disadvantage. The other team kept their promise. They tried not to look too obvious, but left Joey alone on his shots.

Then, the shooting gallery began. Joey put up quite a few shots, but nothing went in. Since he wasn't aware of what was going on, he didn't clue in that he could get closer to the basket and make it easier for himself. My boys kept scoring on his rebounds, and they played much better defense, as they wanted as many chances as possible to get that one assist that mattered the most to us. The other team played their subs, so the lead narrowed to 20 at one point late in the game.

With 5 minutes left, I noticed something about the fans. Without anyone saying anything, the opposition fans started to react every time Joey shot the ball. With every air ball, bounce out, and crazy shot that missed, they 'oohed' and 'awed', like he was on their team. Now that is saying a lot, because our fans were likely outnumbered 10-1 in the stands.

With 3 minutes left, it was evident that everyone in the building wanted Joey to score. I looked back at his parents for their reaction. They are such sweet, loving people. They had lived every moment with him at every game, hoping for a glimmer of something to help him feel better about his efforts. His marks weren't great, he didn't think he had many friends, and there was no other activity that he loved or excelled in more than basketball. Well, at least that's what he seems to think at this age.

God must have been smiling down on us all, as with just over a minute left to play, Joey scored his first and probably only basket of his life in the middle of a game. If a picture had been taken the moment after, you could have easily put the headline "Rural boys shock city boys in playoff game" under the image I witnessed through a lump in my throat so big I couldn't see very well.

The celebration was amazing, as if we had won the national championship or something. I stood and cheered, looked at the whole crowd doing the same, and then looked at Joey's parents. I will never forget the look of sheer joy in their eyes, and the tears streaming down their cheeks. Joey rushed back to play defense faster than ever before, with a look of accomplishment I had so desperately wanted to see in his eyes.

Yeah, we didn't win many games this year, but our team came together for something truly remarkable, and I am so happy with today's accomplishments. Though I'm not sure how I'll afford it at month's end, I bought everyone on the team a milkshake today, and thanked each boy for a great year. We made a little history in a way only we will know about. I will remember this forever, and I hope the boys do too. Joey had his moment in the sun, and better than that, he knows how much his team cares for him. That is so important at age 14.

June 3, 1996

It happened. Kerry and I had our first big fight. I don't know what to do, but I brought my journal to the school with me to write my thoughts down, and cool off a little.

With a baby on the way, I know we are both scared to death of making mistakes as parents. On my side of things, I feel a need to spend a lot of time at the school so I can keep on top of things. An athletic program doesn't run itself. Sometimes I get the feeling that Kerry wonders if I stay here to avoid her. I honestly don't. I've never lied to her about where I have been when I don't come home exactly when she'd like me to get there after work.

To me, it seems like she is being quite unreasonable and selfish. I am not here for me. I am here for my students, and because of that, it means I have a better chance to keep my job. If students quit playing on all of the sports teams after school that will make me look bad. I am only doing all of this for the good of my family.

Kerry thinks I don't do my fair share of work around the house. Usually, I get to those little odd jobs, but many nights when I get home from work, I am so tired that I can't do one more thing. When I got mad at her tonight, I told her I wished I could stay at home all day and watch television. Then I accused her of knowing more about who shot Victor on 'The Young and The Restless' than she knew about me. That comment didn't go over well.

Right as she was going to respond, we had company come over unexpectedly. It was one of our neighbors, named Marilyn. That was my cue to leave. Marilyn is divorcing right now, and I don't like how close Kerry is to her. I think they man-bash when I'm not around.

Quickly, I made up an excuse to be at the school, grabbed my book bad, and headed out.

In my family, I was taught to get some time away to breathe, calm down, and think things through if an argument was getting heated. Now, I feel bad for snapping at Kerry, and mocking that she watches a little bit of soap opera trash on television. It's not what I really wanted to say, but sometimes I feel totally lost when I try to understand why men and women think about the same things so differently. Happy birthday to me.

June 10, 1996

Kerry and I made up our quarrel today. I've agreed to help more with stuff around the house, and she has agreed to speak up sooner if something is wrong instead of letting bad feelings build up until she really lashes out at me. I need to work on that part too.

It's still really early in our marriage, but I think we both are willing to admit when we are wrong at times. I feel like I am wrong more often, but for now we are both winning the game of love, and find a way to make peace that lasts. Well, it lasts at least until the next disagreement.

Sure, I don't know everything about being a perfect husband yet, but I at least try to understand Kerry. She admits that Marilyn is a destructive influence, and that I am nothing like her husband. We have decided that for now while Marilyn is so bitter, Kerry doesn't want to spend time alone with her. If she has something nasty to say about men, she will have to say it in front of me.

August 16, 1996

Triplets? I can't believe this. Kerry delivered today at only 33 weeks. The doctor says sometimes one baby will hide behind the other during the first ultrasound, so we had no idea this was coming. I'm happy, but more overwhelmed by all of this. It was already going to be an adjustment having one more person in our little family, but three? Major changes are coming. I don't want to sound like I am complaining here, as I know children are a gift from God.

Kerry seemed healthy during the pregnancy, and our doctor didn't see the need to run any more tests after the first ultrasound. The last two months were much more difficult, as she was bigger than she thought she would get, but being the sweet guy I am, I didn't EVER make a comment about it. I just figured it meant the baby would be a healthy, strapping boy.

Oh, I guess I was wrong about that too. Our triplets are all girls. I didn't have any girl names floating around in my head, so I guess Kerry will have more of a say on these names! The doctor was nice about all of this, but wondered why Kerry hadn't noticed she was being kicked by three sets of legs, not just one. He'd never seen anyone have triplets that didn't know ahead of time they were coming. Since it was her first, she didn't really know what to expect.

I am trying so hard to be strong for Kerry, as I can tell that she is worried about all of this happening at once. Both of us want to be the best parents we can, and put pressure on ourselves to succeed where our own families weren't perfect. I think we'll be fine eventually. She will need more than just one year before she can take on a teaching job now, I am pretty sure about that.

August 17, 1996

We have named our little girls: Whitney, Brittney, and Courtney. I still can't get over how little they are. At this point the doctors are watching them closely since they were born 3 weeks early and were pretty small. Whitney was 4 lbs. 8 ounces, Brittney was 4 lbs. 2 ounces, and Courtney was 4 lbs. 6 ounces. Can't write more today, I was up all night with Kerry, she had a rough night with feeding this many mouths.

August 18, 1996

Whitney has had some major troubles today. She was sent via helicopter ambulance to a larger hospital. Kerry stayed behind with Brittney and Courtney. Good thing I had some summer holiday left to be with Whitney. Anyway, the problem is with Whitney's lungs. They haven't fully developed yet. She's been struggling to breathe on her own. It's all so frightening right now.

The doctors are only giving her a 50% chance of living. I haven't worked long enough at my job to have full medical benefits yet, so the ride in the helicopter and the stay in the hospital could become a rather excessive bill. I can't worry about that right now, I feel like I need to stay by my baby, and phone her Mom every so often with updates.

2nd Place

September 12, 1996

Whitney is pulling through now, to the relief of all of us, but most especially Kerry. It's been so great getting those two reunited, even if it's still in our local hospital again. I have been so swamped at work. Getting things organized for a new school year is pretty time consuming. Whitney's care was crucial to her survival, but it cost us over $200,000. The hospitals are being patient now (no pun intended), as they know we don't have that kind of money available, but I am not certain how we are going to make good on that bill. Whitney's life is worth that much to me though.

October 3, 1996

I recently met with a banker, and we have financing in place to pay the medical bills, but we have to downsize our home considerably. Kerry and I will just have to make things work with a single level, two-bedroom home for a few years. It's also looking like because of our money situation, we may not have more children later on. I really wanted a son. This news is hard to take.

October 18, 1996

Marilyn came over today after supper was over to see how all of us were doing. She brought a yummy dessert too, and a card. It was unexpected, as no one has a birthday today.

On the inside of the card, she thanked us for being such a good example to her. We are shocked to hear that she has decided not to get a divorce after all. These last few months Kerry actually had a good influence on her, especially when we have been going through so much with our little Whitney. Inspired by how well Kerry treated me, she tried the same thing with her husband, and they are back together and quite happy.

Trust me, I am happier than anyone in this situation. I thought Marilyn would be a cancer that ruined our lives, but it went so much better than that. What a relief!

November 18, 1996

After all that was done for our little Whitney, we can only mourn her loss now. She passed away last night at home. The doctors think her heart failed. The medications and treatment they gave her to assist her lung development and function can sometimes take a toll on the heart. She had lived at home with us for 6 weeks. The tests they gave her all suggested her heart was healthy. Kerry and I are devastated. We still have to pay these medical bills, but now have no child to show for it.

Dad came by the house tonight. He cares but admits he really doesn't know what to do for us. We just have to grieve, heal, and move on somehow, someday. Losing a child is different than losing a partner. It's also harder than when I lost my mother. We expect to see our parents die during our lifetime, but not our own children.

Kerry seems beyond comfort, as for some reason she is blaming herself for Whitney's death. I know this is going to take time to get over, but I don't know how to help Kerry today. I feel so drained, powerless, empty. I hope we find something positive in our lives to help us bounce back from this.

December 24, 1996

I suppose the only way to describe our first Christmas with our children is that it was bittersweet. Brittney and Courtney looked so cute in the pictures I took of our little family by our Christmas tree. We hung a stocking for each of our 3 little girls. I couldn't hold back the tears when I saw Whitney's name and her photo in her stocking. Somehow, all of us will keep part of her with us forever.

I am not overly religious, but when I said our evening prayer, I managed to thank God for all of our little girls, and I told Him I trusted him to watch over my little Whitney, wherever she is now. Kerry and I just sobbed and held each other for a few minutes, until Brittney needed feeding. I still have 2 beautiful girls, and I need to live for them now.

Chapter 11: 1999

Chapter 11: 1999

May 24, 1999

I am a little in shock today because our principal, Doug Smith, retired. I guess this has been in the works for quite awhile, but in secret. His successor has already been announced, and it will be some guy from a few counties away, and his last name is Jones. I think someone said his first name was Chuck. Doug will be hard to replace. He is one of the few administrators I have known who truly had parents, students, and staff happy with him most of the time. That's a tough thing to do.

I asked him if he had any words of wisdom for me, since I hope to have a long, fulfilling career like his. All Doug mentioned was, "Never take things personally when kids behave out of character. It may seem as though they are trying to hurt you, but they are usually just looking for help."

Doug actually apologized to me for what he did to my tires ten years ago. I told him not to worry, as I had felt worse about lying to his face about what had really happened that Halloween night. In the long run, his prank had taught me something. I became a better man from that lesson.

Then, he let me know he was so proud of me for keeping my life together after my Mom had died. That's why he hadn't been too forceful with the cops. He didn't tell anyone but my Dad that he had witnessed me waxing the car windows.

May 28, 1999

I don't believe this. My new boss next year is a guy named Derrick Jones. I completely forgot this guy's middle name because I always called him 'Ralph'. Yup, my biggest, most hated rival on the football field in high school is now going to be my new principal. Should be interesting. I wonder if he's grown up, and less annoying now. I'll call him 'Derrick' to his face, but he will always be 'Ralph' in my heart.

August 26, 1999

We had a great little birthday party for our little girls. Dad and Jennifer both made it out. Alex is too busy with school to come, but he did phone. Jared also phoned. He's in the military now. We took the girls to a petting zoo. They both want a pony now, but our yard is not big enough, and I don't have any idea how we'd afford to feed one more family member. All I could do was promise them that we will come back to zoo as often as possible. They agreed, at least for now. I can tell they were disappointed. At 3 years old, I hope they get over this quickly. Not many people actually have their own ponies for their kids to play on in their own back yard.

September 1, 1999

This year's football team is going to compete well I am sure. We have never had the luxury of a big, fast offensive line before, since we are a small school. I also have some pretty fast kids in our offensive backfield. On defense, we are more of a quick, gang-tackling unit this year. Not lots of size up front, but they play like a pack of lean, hungry wolves. It's fun to watch. My rookies this year are quite intimidated by them in practices. Eventually, I hope that toughens them up.

I guess that's not totally true. I have one rookie this year that is not intimidated by anything. His name is Kendon. I didn't catch his last name, but I do recall having to reel him in a few times today. Kendon is not the fastest or tallest, but he is likely the strongest, most determined player I have ever seen to this point in my coaching career.

After he injured two of my starters during tackling drills, I pulled him aside and told him he's making the team, and that he can still impress me by saving some of his zip for the opponents we face this year. I hope he can keep quiet about that. Kendon may actually start at outside linebacker for me this year. Being able to start a rookie is quite a tribute to him.

September 15, 1999

I saw a financial planner today, just to see how we are doing, what we can realistically expect for a lifestyle, savings, retirement etc. With debts like ours, it would be easy to get discouraged and give up on all of our dreams. We are paying minimums on everything just so we have the money to eat. My teaching salary will increase each year as I gain more experience, but once that tops off, I wonder if it will ever feel like enough.

Anyway, the good news is, we may be able to afford to have another child. Kerry and I both would like that. I want to have a son, and Kerry hopes I get my wish. I will have to work in the potato fields during the summers to generate a little more income. I did that sort of work when I was a teen, so I know how already. I don't mind that because it will keep me strong, and hopefully be a good example for my sports teams that I coach.

Speaking of my team, we have not been scored on this season yet. That quick little defense we have is ferocious, and plays well as a unit. We have not played the Lions yet, but I think we can compete with them next month. I can't wait. Ralph is keeping his nose out of my business so far. The budget for P.E. and sports teams has been kept intact. That's a comfort to me because when principals change, sometimes principles do too. Ralph likes winning, so he's making sure he's doing his part to support the program.

Eddy is still playing in Green Bay these days. At the pace he is gaining yardage, he will break a few NFL records. Staying healthy enough will be the trick. He seems prone to ankle sprains. Some things never change, that's how he met Hope officially. I can tell Eddy feels a little sorry for Kerry and me because of our debt struggles. He offered to help with some, but I turned him down. I'm not too proud to accept help. I know his situation better than it seems he does, so I can't take his money.

Eddy has no career to fall back on, and he really needs to save his money for when football is over. I don't know who would hire him. He has not been a great employee as a football player. Ability has kept him going, but his work ethic is slipping, and he is getting pretty conceited. Some of the sports writers say his selfishness with money issues has really become a problem for other players on his own team. That's too bad. I thought Eddy would be different than this. Fame changes people I guess. I can only hope that were I in his shoes that I wouldn't have let that happen to me.

October 18, 1999

We played the Lions this week at home, and we beat them 28-27. It was a thriller to watch, but not a thriller to coach. We were up 28-14 with 3 minutes to go, and we almost gave the game away. The Lions took advantage of a pass that was tipped at the line on a 3rd and 8 play. While protecting the lead, I guess it was my fault for calling a pass play. They scored on the next play from the 30-yard line on a cute little double reverse. Our defense over pursued the original hand-off, and we only had one guy stay back. He was easily blocked, so that score was made without much trouble. That made the score 28-21.

On our next possession, we went three and out, and kicked it back to the Lions with 50 seconds left to go. Our kick coverage was terrible, and they got a huge return. We should have pinned them at their 15 yard-line, but we ended up allowing them to make it to our own 26 yard-line instead. Three plays later they got a touchdown. The only reason we won? They got greedy and went for a two-point conversion instead. I think they were counting on their momentum to punch it in, but their pass attempt was batted away, and we preserved the win. Kendon, my star, rookie linebacker, was in the quarterbacks face and forced an early throw. He got 2 sacks and 10 tackles in today's game.

Ralph was there today too. I don't know why, but I had a strange feeling around him. He appeared glad we won, but it's hard to explain how it felt to have him cheering from the seats behind me. Maybe I should call him Derrick or Mr. Jones like everyone else does.

October 31, 1999

I can't remember the exact day of practice last week, but something disturbed me that I had to act on after practice. I have always counted on team leaders to inspire the other boys to take practice, training, and conditioning seriously. This year, Kendon has been that leader. Having a rookie in this role is so refreshing. The older boys have a hard time holding their own with him because of his enthusiasm. Well at least that has been the case most days.

One day this week, I noticed that Kendon was much more quiet about things, and wasn't running with the speed and intensity I was used to. I let it go throughout practice, hoping he'd kick himself into line. He didn't. Now, he was not a destructive force either, but I could just tell by looking at him that something wasn't right. I got after him toward the end of practice. He simply replied he was giving all he had today, so I left him alone.

After practice was over, I asked to see him for a minute privately. He came to me looking like he was afraid of being scolded or something, and I quickly requested that he not be afraid of anything I had to say. I asked him why he had so little to give today, and his response broke my heart. He mentioned how hungry he was, and that he hadn't eaten much for a few days. All he managed to get was the food his friends were thinking of throwing away during lunchtime at school.

I was then almost too afraid to ask why he had no lunch, but I needed that truth. He broke down and cried. He told me about his Father's drinking and gambling addictions. His Mother had checked herself in at the psych ward because the financial problems the family had really hurt her, and sent her into a deep depression. Kendon was trapped in the middle. He had no real Mother influence, a dysfunctional Father, and no end of his hunger in sight.

Obviously, Kendon's story caught me off guard. I started to encourage him a little, but I knew he needed more than that. Next, I asked him to come with me to the office, where I called Kerry on the phone. I asked if it would be OK to serve one more person tonight for supper. Then I thought better of it and said two more people would be there, so Kendon could eat until he was full. Kerry hesitated at first, since she knows how tight our budget is at this point. She agreed, and Kendon met me at the house an hour later.

Kendon was a perfect gentleman, and a gracious guest in our home. He did the dishes with me after, and that part was his idea. I asked if he needed to let his Dad know where he was, and he informed me that his Dad would probably not be home before 10 or 11. So, that gave us more time to talk. Kerry had some counseling courses at university, and she visited with Kendon and I after we tucked the girls into bed. Watching her passionately help someone with matters of the heart makes me love her more each time I see her in action.

We let Kendon do most of the talking. He had been through some rough times, and needed to tell someone. I think he felt safe to do that with us because we explained how we respected his strengths, and felt he had enough skill to get what he wants out of life. After he had told us all that was going wrong at home, we simply asked him what he was going to do about it. At first he was a little surprised. He must have thought we were going to tell him how to fix it, but that's not what he needed to hear. Thank heaven Kerry knew this about truly helping someone. I wanted to give him a bunch of advice, but Kerry made sure the conversation went the right way.

After our question, Kendon thought for a long time. He cried a bit, brainstormed for ideas awhile, and eventually settled on a solution he could live with. He determined that the neglect he was suffering was unjust, and that there were legal reasons why he could have social services remove him from the home. That didn't seem right though because he loved his Dad. He didn't want to hurt him with the embarrassment of losing his only son.

Kendon realized though that he had asked his Dad to change, but his Dad had failed to do that. He determined that he would let his Dad know that he would report the neglect to the proper authorities if things didn't get better. Kendon wanted to give his Dad a chance to change first because he loved him, but he also wanted to let him know he was ready to do something for himself if his Dad wouldn't shape up.

I asked Kendon if he needed help explaining this to his Dad, but he said he'd do all of this himself. As usual, I was amazed by his toughness. Kerry also gave my arm a slight tug, and gave me that look which meant I needed to mind my own business. I suppose I need to learn that. Glad I have a smart wife.

Later, I drove Kendon home, and dropped him off at an empty, depressing place that looked so unkempt. Kendon's home looked like it had been beautiful at one time. Now, the garden was overgrown with weeds, everything looked filthy, and the weeds were so tall in the front that you could barely tell where the front window of the house was. It was 10:00, and his Dad was still not back from wherever it was he'd gone to that night.

Just before he got out of my car, I thanked Kendon for being so strong, and a good leader on the football team. I offered to talk to him again if he ever needed that from someone who cared. He thanked me for that, but assured me that he had a plan now, and that he would just live it. As I pulled away from his house I watched him walk toward the door. He picked up his cat, and gave it a big hug. He then held it up high. I couldn't hear the words he spoke, but he had a smile on his face.

I got a feeling he'd be fine, though that seemed to be so unbelievable and improbable because his surroundings were in such disarray. Driving was hard because I had a large lump in my throat as I headed home. How blessed I felt right then for having the Dad I did.

Chapter 11: 1999

November 20, 1999

I can't believe the parallels between this season and the football season I had as a teen when we almost won the state championship. The only real difference is that we beat the Lions in the regular season this year. The state championship results were the same though. We had a lead that we lost in the end. The game itself was not pretty. We only scored off the Lion's turnovers in the first half. They got even, and then some in the second half. It's too painful to share all of the details of this game, so I will not go into it.

What bothers me the most though, is the look Ralph gave me at the end. Every other time we've won or lost a game, he as always said the words 'good game coach'. This time, he simply disappeared. I had the best team I have ever enjoyed at this school. I spent extra time working with some of my key players after the regular practices were over. I don't know what more I could have done for them this season.

These young men are going to do well in life because they work so hard, they are aware of their limits, strengths, and weaknesses. Being that self-aware this early in their lives is even a great example to me. Again, I know I have done all I can for these boys. They know I care about them as individuals, not just as pawns in some game where I want to have the glory of a championship for me.

Ralph seems to want more. I think he's disappointed that we can't win the big game. He won it all as a player when he was a teen, so he knows how good that feels. I will never forget what a dirty player he and his teammates were though. Whether he expects dirty play from my boys or not, I won't go that route. These young men of mine deserve to win honorably. That's the best way to ensure they do well in real life later on.

Chapter 12: 2000

January 1, 2000

Since I am still typing this today on my 486 computer with Windows 95, I guess I can safely say that the Y2K bug has indeed been fixed. Their was doubt in my mind about this, and I admit, I did stash a 3-month supply of toilet paper, food, and water in the root cellar last fall just in case.

Christmas 1999 was great. Everyone met at Dad and Jennifer's for Christmas Eve and Christmas Day. Jared and Alex are both married now, and have a son each. Wow, time sure has gone by quickly. It's hard to believe they are raising kids now too. Kerry and I were thrilled to announce that we are expecting again for September. We are both praying we have only one baby this time. We also both hope it's a boy.

I have to admit, now that I am a parent and a teacher I see the wisdom in maintaining a marriage relationship with dating. When I was a teen, I know it wasn't fun taking care of younger siblings while Dad and Jennifer went out on Fridays. As I consider it carefully though, I know it wasn't every Friday. It was probably only once or twice a month.

The benefit it provided to them was pretty clear. They always talked things through peacefully, and because we as kids saw that consistently, we knew they loved each other. Their private time away always seemed to be followed by happy times for the whole family. It was as if they rededicated themselves each time to being better for us. I never lived with doubts of their unity or love.

As a teacher, I can see the value of that as I watch my students from broken or nearly broken homes. I can tell which students are suffering from that before I know the family situation. Kerry and I manage to go on dates now too, and I guess Dad was right about this. Life wasn't so bad when I was a kid. I hope to follow Dad's example even when my girls are teens.

It's been weird not coaching basketball this season. King Ralph brought in a new science teacher last fall that is better at basketball, and he replaced me as basketball coach. He assures me that I will have other extra-curricular assignments later on to compensate for my increase in time off. I find this a little hard to take as I already do so much for the school compared to many other staff members. I am not complaining, but fail to see Ralph's logic sometimes. I do what he asks because he is my boss, but I have to admit I don't go out of my way to befriend him.

February 4, 2000

Dad helped me nurse our 1986 Dodge Caravan back to health. I was so sure it wouldn't run again. I wish I had more of a knack for fixing vehicles. Without Dad, I would have been completely lost. We had to put in a new transmission and exhaust system. I've never had such dirty hands. It will take a full week to get them completely clean again I think. The new engine is has 3-year warrantee, and so does the transmission we just put in. I hope this thing lasts a long time. We can't afford anything newer than this right now. At least the previous owners made sure the body had no dents or rust. That's amazing for a van that is 14 years old.

Last week Eddy's team, the Tennessee Titans lost in the Super Bowl. He made headlines for criticizing his QB and his coaches afterward. I have to admit that I can't side with him on this one. The things he said really should be kept private in the locker room. He may make it hard to stay employed in the NFL if he keeps doing things like this. Having great ability is one thing, but upsetting team chemistry is another. I hope we see an apology from Eddy on the sports channels soon.

On a more positive note, 5 of the players from my football team were scouted to play college football, and each of them has some choices about where to attend school next year. This makes a total of 23 players that have been selected from our school since I began coaching here. Great feeling to know I have given them some positive preparation.

May 27, 2000

I wonder what Ralph is up to now. I have been assigned to teach more classes, but with fewer prep periods. I am also supposed to start a jazz choir because there is interest, and the band teacher is already doing a jazz band for his extra-curricular assignment. I haven't done much with music since my university days. I know it will all come back to me. It's not that I don't want to do this, but I am pretty busy already. I hoped I would have more time with my family at this point in my life.

Ralph went back and looked at my university transcripts noticed that I had some coursework with jazz choir. I will be provided with a piano player, since one of the parents volunteered to help with this. We have no choice but to meet at noon because sports take priority after school. I can only be in one place at a time once during football and track and field. Ralph says he will consider making jazz choir available during regular school time if enough students join.

September 13, 2000

It's a girl! Kerry delivered our little Sarah Jane this morning at 8:39. What a sweetie she is. She hardly fusses, and when she does, it's almost like she is trying to be polite about it. We have known since June she would be a girl. We have named her after my Mom. Not sure if she will want to be known as Sarah or Jane. We'll wait until she is old enough to choose. I like both names. Of course I was hoping for a boy, but I can still teach my girls to love sports with their music.

Preparing to teach my jazz choir has been a challenge, but a fun process at the same time. I realize now that I made a choice to enjoy music simply because my Mom really liked it, and it always seems to remind me of her.

Now, I am a little sad that I have let some of my talent go for so many years. I get so wrapped up in sports I forget about this side of me. If I had known I would be teaching jazz choir now, I may have lived the last few years differently.

We had our first rehearsals last week. The songs I chose were a little too challenging for a first year choir, so I will have to switch to some new ones. There hasn't been a choir of any kind in our school for over 20 years. So basic singing concepts will have to be covered first.

Ralph did it to me again this year. He made a major change in my assignment a week before school started. Our school lost a few teachers to retirement, including our school counselor. I will now be working half days as a counselor, and the other half as the high school PE teacher. Someone else is taking the 7-9 PE for me.

This change is not so bad actually. I already find that kids and I get along well one on one, so in some ways this is a natural progression. When I think of how many students I have helped with athletic scholarship applications, I am also comforted to know that I already have some experience with my new job duties. I am not used to the amount of paperwork that will have to be done though. That's going to be what keeps me busier this year. Well, that and starting a brand new jazz choir.

It could be worse I suppose. At least I have a genuine love for doing the things that will make me busier. Had King Ralph assigned me to teach sewing or history, I think I would have refused and made a formal complaint to his bosses. He is lucky that he picked something I could handle. Well, I guess I am the lucky one really.

November 14, 2000

Wow, lots happening this year, and I haven't had the time to write in my journal. Though I knew ahead of time this would be a building year for my football team, it still hurts that we missed the playoffs. The boys gave their all, but we didn't have the strength or speed this year to make a run for the state championship. Though disappointed, I am relieved on the other hand.

Because of Jazz choir, the new counseling assignment, and a new baby with Kerry on maternity leave, I am quietly grateful we had a shorter football season this year. I think next year we will be in the playoffs again though.

Chapter 13: 2001

Chapter 13: 2001

April 30, 2001

To my surprise, our jazz choir has done very well. When kids want something badly enough, they'll work like crazy. I promised we'd take a musical trip at least 5 hours away from home if we could get a Superior Rating at the music festival in the city. Not only did my students get that rating, but they were awarded with the best choir award as well. We performed in the Showcase Of Excellence at the end of the week. Our trip was paid for by the festival committee, so I didn't need to use any school funds for that.

As for me, I am enjoying music again. It's been a great healer for me, though the more I get over Mom, the closer I feel to her. Peaceful, but odd at the same time. I believe what my counselor told me now. I had doubts before.

King Ralph was kind enough to get me some music conductor training. It was paid for out of the professional development funds. I didn't realize what a rush it would be to lead a choir. Making music together is a different experience than smacking another football team around on the field. No one loses in music. Everyone gets to contribute. When it comes together and sounds good, we all win. I will have to work hard to shake free from this sweet, loving mentality in time for next September when football start up again!

We got our pictures in the local newspaper. The town still seems in shock that their PE teacher can lead a choir. I am not really that good at leading. Honestly, I am still so new at this; I wish the focus would just stay on the kids. I am enthusiastic though, and my love of music seems to be inspiring them. I suppose that's good enough for now.

September 13, 2001

Our little Sarah Jane turned one year old today. The twins have always referred to her as Janie. Not the Jane I was hoping for, but she responds to it so well, and it suits her. I guess this name will stick as her preferred name. She has the most adorable little curls in her hair right now. She tries to sing, and bounces up and down whenever music is playing. Brittney and Courtney are such fun big sisters for her too.

I was talking about Brittney and Courtney the other day, and referred to them as 'the twins'. I can't remember whom I was talking to, but they were surprised we call them twins, since they are triplets who survived the death of their sister. Discussing all of this again was painful, but I understood what was being asked.

When we were grieving Whitney's death, Kerry and I decided to live for our girls who were still with us. We didn't want them to be reminded of our loss every time we referred to them, or to think that somehow they were of lesser value to us than Whitney. Instead, we simply tell our girls that there is one more angel in heaven who looks after them, and that she looks just like them too. It seems to be fine.

I know there must be a heaven. There has to be. I feel like my Mom is nearby some days. Grandpa Palmer is close too when I am coaching a big game. Anyway, when we all get to heaven my girls will be reunited and I will refer to them as triplets. For now, I love and care for my twins.

Kerry enjoyed the full year off for her maternity leave. She gets to go back and teach Home Economics now, because that's the position that is available to her. She's happy about that part, but has truly hated leaving her little Janie behind each morning. If only we had less debt, we could afford to have Kerry home longer.

The van is making funny noises again. I think the brakes are about ready for new pads or something. Dad says I should learn to do them myself. Guess we'll see if that happens. (I have my doubts.)

Ralph is at it again. This year he has gotten some parents together to coach boy's volleyball. I have nothing against the sport, but for a school our size; it's a stupid idea. How am I supposed to run a decent football program if half my athletes switch sports? It remains to be seen how many boys switch out of football. King Ralph has given them until tomorrow to decide. I don't understand this man. I know he wants us to win in football. This move is so irrational. I could almost understand it if parents had pressured him, but it was the other way around.

September 20, 2001

The damage is over. I only lost 6 players to volleyball. One of them was my starting 6' 7" defensive tackle. He wants to save his body for a possible basketball scholarship, and feels football may be too risky of a sport to play. I understand this move, and we'll be fine, once I get someone else in there who knows what he's doing. The other 5 players were also some of my taller players, but they weren't beefy enough for football, so we will manage without them.

Chapter 13: 2001

I suppose I dodged a bullet somewhat, but I hate to think what will happen over the next few years. I won't worry. I just need to focus on what I have, and take these boys as far as I can. So far we have a 2-2 record. I knew going in that this year we would be average. My offence is scoring enough points, but our defense is lacking in speed and size. We're getting pushed around too much.

I recently told my boys about my new philosophy about life, and how it affects our team, and the individuals on it. I am urging them to replace the 3 'c' words, with 3 'g' words. In life it's very easy to criticize, complain, or compare our own lives to that of others. I want us to replace these with being genuine, grateful, and gritty. The boys all seem to understand why being gritty is one of my goals. I had to explain why being grateful makes us appreciate things, and live happier than always wanting what can't be, or by dwelling too much on what hasn't happened yet.

They also wondered about being genuine, and I told them in life, like in football, we can't hide behind our mistakes. The opposition always finds us. We have to be honest with ourselves, and fix where we are weak. A player who tells me he knows his job, and is too conceited to ask for help, and then fails on the field because of it, lets his team down because of his own pride.

Honestly, this group of kids may not be the greatest team I have ever coached, but as men in the real world, they will succeed because they have heart, and they are willing to listen and learn.

Most notably, I have to talk about Kendon. He's a senior this year, and was the brightest spot on the team. Right now, he leads the league in sacks, tackles for loss, special team tackles, and interceptions by a linebacker. Pretty impressive resume.

That's not his greatest achievement though. Last weekend he invited me to his home to pay me back for the dinner I had fed him such a long time ago. He told me he was a good cook, because he had taken cooking classes at school. To my surprise, he wanted the whole family to come. The house I had dropped him off at two years ago was still in my memory, and as I recalled that memory, I doubted this would be a good idea. However, I agreed to it because he was so persistent.

When Kerry and I got there with our girls, I was shocked to see the yard and home improvements. It was as though a professional crew had come in, like on those TV shows where they fix something up for someone. We went inside and saw a house that was spotless, the food smelled great, and there was Kendon, beaming with joy because we had agreed to come over.

I hadn't heard much about his parents. Kendon had just continued to impress on the field, and hadn't said a word about home, because I think he wanted that kept private. We ate a wonderful meal. Kendon had prepared a meal that featured Chicken Alfredo with Tortellini, the best garlic toast I had ever had, and a Caesar salad that Kerry thought tasted as good as her Mom's did.

The evening just kept getting better though. After dinner, the kids all went to play in the basement, and Kendon offered to watch them for us. His parents, Walter and Carol, wanted to talk to Kerry and I. They told us how grateful they were that we had taken Kendon in that night, and for helping him to feel like he had some control of his own life. Walter explained the confrontation the night when I dropped Kendon off 2 years before.

Hearing his own son ask for change, but also that he had a course of action prepared if he didn't get results really captured Walter's attention. He had lost his job, and had been living with a false sense of peace, because he didn't have a boss to nag him anymore. At first, Walter admitted he was resentful, and a little bit mad at Kerry and I for putting ideas in Kendon's head. It wasn't until Walter saw Kendon cry that he softened enough, and realized he better listen. Kendon explained that he did love his Dad; but that he was prepared to leave him if staying meant he'd suffer too much.

Walter got professional help for drinking and gambling because he couldn't bear the thought of his son disowning him or reporting him to social services. It was a difficult process, but within 6 months, Walter was sober, had a new job, and was living a very stable life. Carol felt she could trust him, and she returned home as well. She had been living with her sister, who lived 10 hours away. Carol had missed Kendon, but knew he needed to stay in the school he was at, just to stay close to a good man like Coach Workman.

Walter figured his strength to change came because he was a religious man. He feared that God would not be pleased with him for being so unsupportive to Kendon and Carol. That was the one thing that kept playing in his mind, and almost forced him to make changes while he was in rehab. Walter and Carol thanked us for all

Chapter 13: 2001

we did, but we didn't feel right about that. It was Kendon who had done the work. All that he had done was his own idea, not ours.

December 23, 2001

I forgot to write in here at the end of football season. It wasn't a memorable year on the score sheet, but we did have the distinction of being the only team that beat the Lions. They went on to win everything else though. I did overhear a couple of my boys saying they are switching to volleyball next year because we missed the playoffs in football this year. I couldn't tell who they were, as it was by accident that I even heard them talking.

My choir is really rocking. I agree that last sentence is a bit of a paradox or an oxymoron. The new band teacher, Mrs. Pimentel asked us to join in with their Christmas Concert this year. We sang an arrangement of O Holy Night with the band, and then performed a section of the Hallelujah Chorus from Handel's Messiah with piano accompaniment. My favorite though was when we sang You're A Mean One Mr. Grinch. Yeah, I know, I am supposed to love the classics more, but I like having fun.

Mrs. Pimentel asked me to join her jazz band and play piano. She heard me messing around on it the other day. I had to turn her down. I don't have the time for one more thing right now, though I know I would love it. I suppose we are lucky that in our little community we have enough teachers to run a band, jazz band, and jazz choir. That's a rare thing even in some bigger schools.

December 28, 2001

Today was the funeral for my Grandpa Workman. He was alone for a long time before he died. He wanted to remarry, but every time he spent time with ladies his age, it just made him miss Grandma more, and he knew there would never be anyone as wonderful as she was. He kept saying it wouldn't be fair for a new woman to live in her shadow all the time.

For me, it never gets easier to let go of someone who dies. I was just as sad today as when Grandma Workman died. So, to help me to feel better about all of this, I will do now what I did then. So I never forget him and what he meant to me, I will write the good in him that I saw so he lives forever in my memory.

Grandpa Workman could fix anything that was broken. People

from miles around would come to him for help. He was a short man, but very strong. He always grinned as he puttered around the garage, his shop in his basement, and his ham radio tower in his back yard.

One week, when I was 8 years old, I remember staying at his house when Mom and Dad went on a holiday without us kids. Grandpa figured out that I was scared of the dark when it was bedtime. So, on the first night, he let me sleep in his basement with one light on. Each night, I got to use a dimmer and dimmer light, until at the end of the week I was used to it, and slept in total darkness. I got used to it, and haven't ever been scared of the dark since.

Grandpa had a bit of a temper, and Grandma Workman would sometimes tease him for his lack of patience. He could get very mad at the world sometimes, but he was always a perfect gentleman around her. He passed that love and respect for girls on to Dad and to me.

I just know that Grandpa can see me every day now. Hopefully I am living the way he'd like me to because I know he'll kick my butt in heaven if I don't. For now, I am going to miss his strong handshake, the way he giggled when it was time to eat dessert, and for how much he loved to feed birds, squirrels, and small children in parks.

Chapter 14: 2002

Chapter 14: 2002

January 21, 2002

With Kerry and I both working again, we have paid off our credit cards, and have now qualified for financing an addition for our house. We could sure use the extra space. We are going to add a garage on the south side of the house, put two bedrooms above it, and then knock out a wall to expand the size of our living room. Once the weather warms up, we will get started on the project.

Yesterday, Eddy starred in the St. Louis Rams victory in the NFC Championship game. They beat the Philadelphia Eagles 29-24, and play in the Super Bowl in 2 weeks. I will definitely be cheering for the Rams in this one. I am a little choked that Drew Bledsoe lost his starting job to Tom Brady, due to an injury. Brady has played well of course, but if coaches don't reward players with loyalty after injuries, I wonder if that will have a negative impact on a player giving his all. I guess time will tell.

February 3, 2002

Eddy played so well today, but it wasn't his team's day. New England won the game. This is two Super Bowls where Eddy has played well but still saw his team lose the game. He was vocal again about not getting the ball thrown his way. Sad to say he just needs to shut up and get ready for next year. Comments like that in any other profession would cost a person his job.

April 23, 2002

Work on our addition to our house finally started today. It took awhile to get the contractors in place for it. I love the new floor plan for the upstairs. We also needed a garage for those cold mornings when we are trying to start the van. Our 1986 Caravan is still working but it may need a heart transplant soon.

May 4, 2002

I am totally stunned, but our house burned down today. The Fire Chief investigated, and he says it was clearly started by faulty wiring in the electrical system in the addition.

It gets worse. There is an argument about whether our insurance company will cover us, or whether the builder's insurance will have to. The only good news besides the safety of my journal is that our whole family is fine. We were all away from the house today for various reasons. I don't know what more to say. I am so devastated. This journal I write in is now my last remaining possession, other than the clothes I am wearing today, and my little van that acts like it is about to die too.

Kerry and the girls are all so strong today. The tears have been flowing all evening, and yet they are already planning in their minds how they will move on, have even better lives later when we get a different house to live in. Funny, I am the man; I need to be the strong one, yet today I am the one leaning on them. Luckily, I married well and have the best girls a father could ask for.

I am glad this journal was with me this week in the car. Usually, I leave it at home beside my bed. I took it to work to show a little bit of it to some students. In classes I have been explaining how journaling can help us to mark our own personal progress in areas like physical, emotional, and mental fitness.

June 12, 2002

Am I being punished for something? I can't understand our family's luck with things. After all the years we paid down high medical bills, and now when we were just starting to think we'd make it, and have a bigger, better house – it burns to the ground, and no insurance company is willing to help because of technicalities with the policies.

I have seen lawyers and business regulating agencies about this problem. Everyone says we are entitled to nothing because of the way our insurance policy was drawn up. Apparently this is some type of glitch that they encouraged me to be aware of in the future. What good does that do me right now? I didn't know the rules of insurance changed during a renovation, and that I needed to inform my insurance company about the addition. I would have only been paying $5 more per month for the coverage I needed.

So, this glitch is costing me about $230,000. The only good news I got today is that Dad has some money stashed away for a rainy day. We can use it as a down payment to rebuild, but for now we have to find somewhere to rent, and there isn't much available here.

In the meantime, Dad is also letting us live in his basement. His renter moved out 3 months ago. We will be squished. Who am I kidding? We don't have any furniture now.

Chapter 14: 2002

July 14, 2002

    Kerry and I have been having trouble while living at my Dad's house. Most of the time, things go great, but I think living under the same roof with three generations causes stress. We get to move into a rental in time for the new school year though, so at least the end of this is near.

Chapter 15: 2005-2007

Chapter 15: 2005-2007

July 25, 2005

I am a little in shock today, but know I did the right thing. We had Eddy and Hope come to visit these last few days. Now that he isn't playing professional football anymore, he can do what he wants, he can go places, he can visit old friends and all that. Eddy was talking tough like things were great in his life. He claimed to have his choice of many places for work. I had no reason to doubt him, because he's usually told me the truth.

He was worn out from a day at the golf course, and needed some rest, so he went back to the hotel kind of early in the evening. Kerry and the girls were all gone shopping, so Hope ended up at my house by herself when I came home from work.

When I came in Hope was lying on our couch watching the television, with a box of tissues beside her. When I entered the room, I could tell she was crying, so I asked her what was wrong. With broken words, she leveled with me that Eddy had no work lined up, and that his gambling debts were likely going to cost him every bit of money he had tried to save for life after football. She also said he was drinking more heavily as soon as he retired, and that his doctors were already concerned about his liver. Again, I was shocked to hear all of this because Eddy had always hidden this type of thing from me, and the media.

What happened next really upset me. Hope had heard rumors that Kerry had been struggling with depression issues. That part was true, but what she didn't know was that Kerry had faced that openly, and done so much better after some herbal treatment, mineral supplements and exercise.

Thinking she'd find me at a weak moment in my marriage, Hope made a pass at me. She asked me to leave everything and be with her. She told me she'd hidden some of Eddy's money for a rainy day, but that he didn't even know it was missing. She had invested it well, and now had a large nest egg, but wanted to share it with someone stable and loving who wasn't drunk all the time. She wanted to keep telling me how badly Eddy was treating her, but I stopped her. I didn't think it was my business, as she admitted he was not abusive, just neglectful and self-absorbed.

However, there I stood, beside the girl I thought I liked all these years. She still looked great, but I couldn't believe my ears. I absolutely refused her, and told her to leave, or I would tell Eddy everything. She seemed disappointed, but didn't want him to know. She withdrew her request, and slinked back onto the couch and cried again.

I asked her how long she had wanted out of her marriage. She informed me things had been rough for a long time, but she had stayed for the money and security of a fun, fast-paced life. Now that it looked like the fun was over, and the money was certainly not going to be as good as it had been, she wanted out. To Hope's surprise, I let her know that even though Eddy had changed so much, he had still been good to me, and that I couldn't hurt him or my own family by running off with her.

She didn't like hearing what I said next, but I let her know she was just being a greedy opportunist, and that she'd end up hurting many people, including herself in the process if she didn't start living differently. I told her that she needed to stick by her choice of marriage partner, and take care of Eddy now, since he had truly done a good job of taking care of her for so long. This love and care for him is probably going to require some type of rehabilitation.

I am so glad I stayed strong for my family. I promised Hope I would stay quiet about all of this if I had clear evidence that she had come clean about her hidden money, and if she'd quit making a play for other sober men. I think she was surprised to see my loyalty to Eddy, despite the fact I had always been a little jealous of him.

On one hand, I see what motivated Hope, and understand a little of how lonely she must have felt all those years when Eddy was in the limelight, but so rarely home. What offended me was why she thought I would have even considered leaving my family for her. For now, I don't want Hope and Eddy to come around as much anymore. I don't need to be mixed up in their problems. The last thing I mentioned to Hope as she left my home was that no success would ever compensate for failure in her home. She seemed to understand that.

August 17, 2005

As of now, all of my grandparents have died. Today was Grandma Palmer's funeral. I was asked to play her favorite song on the piano. She loved the tune 'Danny Boy'. She used to sing that song with Grandpa Palmer all the time.

Once when he was asked to sing that song as a solo at one of

Chapter 15: 2005-2007

his friend's funerals, he got so choked up that he couldn't sing. She got up and helped him finish. They harmonized so well, and I will always remember how they looked while singing. They were so in love that like they were still newly-weds.

Grandma loved to dance, and she always dressed so well. No matter what, she wanted to look her best. At first glance, people may have looked at her and thought she was so prim and proper that she wouldn't get her hands dirty.

Not my grandma. Though she carried herself like dignified royalty, she kept a very clean home and a beautiful garden. She baked chocolate chip cookies for her grandchildren every time she knew we were coming over. I have never tasted a better cookie anywhere else. That is probably because her secret ingredient was love.

March 14, 2007

What GREAT news! All of the efforts to raise money for our new football field and track facilities are paying off. It was announced at my staff meeting today that development has been approved. The field that has sat vacant beside the existing facilities will become the new football field, and the present football field and track will become the spot where we develop the locations for the field events like shot put, long jump, etc. This way, while we wait for things to be built, we still can use what we have without interruption.

There is a committee in charge of choosing a name for it when it is built. I think leaving the name the same is fine. Country Hills High School Athletic Park seems to sum it up for me. Work on the project won't start until next year, and it's expected to take between 18 months and two years to complete.

More details are coming out now about Eddy's retirement from the NFL two years ago. I think it was forced on him. He became a trash-talker more than a player. He was linked to steroid use, but never proven absolutely guilty. He was known as a troublemaker and someone who harmed good feelings among teammates. He made himself a ton of money in his prime, the last 4 seasons he wasn't a dominant player anymore.

I wish he would have just been a little kinder to people, less into showcasing, and stayed clear of the drugs and stuff. It's sad to see his career end on a downer like this. He broke a few important records during his career though, so I guess that's a highlight.

2nd Place

September 18, 2007

I guess I better start today by apologizing to Mom for not writing so much these past couple of years. Kerry, the girls and I are living in a new house on the lot where our old one burned down. Carpentry has never been a skill of mine. My family has been pretty patient with me, as I have attempted to build walls in the basement, and create bedrooms, playrooms, and washrooms.

Over the last few years I have become close friends with Tony from our hardware store. He has been so patient with me, and helped me learn quite a bit about finishing my house myself, because we simply can't afford to hire all of the trades people needed to complete the basement. Half of it is still unfinished, but we have enough bedrooms for everyone for now, so I may just leave it alone for a while.

Tony's son Andy is playing quarterback for the junior football team this coming season. I hear he is very good already. I guess I will have to see what he is like when he is old enough to play on my high school team.

On the present high school football scene, we lost the championship game last November. It's hard to write about coming so close all the time. I really hate losing. I guess that's my excuse for not writing very often this last while.

It was my pleasure to coach a kid named Logan O'Brien during his last two seasons of high school ball. That kid could run, he could find a hole, he could hit the open spots so hard, and it would take 3 or 4 guys to bring him down whenever he carried the football. It isn't often to find a kid that young with such vision for the game, or a sixth sense to know where to run next to find the open areas in a defense.

Logan was another young man who I spent time with after practices were over. His dad lives so far away, because his parents are divorced. Divorce is all too common in the world, but in our little town, it is not as common. I have gotten the feeling that Logan felt like he was looked down on because of who he was, and for not having a father at home.

My opinion of Logan was much different. I thought he commanded respect because he had such determination to be his best all the time. He wasn't a troublemaker or an outcast among his peers. He was simply a fun-loving young man who chose to smile instead.

Chapter 15: 2005-2007

About the only thing I helped him with, was simplifying his life a little so he could focus on one thing at a time. He was so good at everything; he wanted to do it all. He needed to figure out that it's not possible to do everything well all the time. Sometimes, it's OK to do fewer things better, and then wait to take on something new after the first things are mastered.

I would not be surprised to see Logan as a successful businessperson, or teacher. He is so personable, and leads by example. I will miss having him on the team this year.

Something else happened this year that was probably long overdue. Kerry mentioned that it was becoming more difficult for her and I to keep our relationship on solid ground, because I was giving more and more at work, and reaching out to so many students at risk. I was not aware she was worried about this. Friday night date nights were being cancelled too often, and she was starting to wonder if I valued her.

I know this is not the first time Kerry has felt like this in our marriage. The seasons come and go. Sometimes I am totally swamped, others I am a little more at ease and give more of myself to her and the family. When the same old problems keep coming up, I wonder if she thinks I am deliberately doing things to harm her, or to make her doubt how much I love her.

It took some adjusting on my end to pull back a lot from my boys lately. I didn't completely stop helping, but I made sure that I had my small calendar in my pocket all the time, with date nights highlighted so I would never book myself during nights I needed to be with Kerry. It's a lot easier to say you're too busy for someone or something, when you already have a firm commitment to be somewhere else. I am glad Kerry has been patient, yet demanding about us having our time together too.

The longer I am with Kerry, the more she draws me in. It still is a thrill to know that someone so beautiful, smart, and capable of showing such love wants to share all of that with little old me. I get so focused on my goals at times, and I forget some of the little things.

August 7, 2007

This weekend I let Kerry know how much I love her in a way that I think meant a lot to her. First, I made sure she had no plans.

Then, I had the girls all stay at Dad's for the weekend. I arranged for a Hawaiian band to play some music for us at a secluded resort that we actually stayed at on our way home from our honeymoon.

I hired a massage therapist to come up too and give her some treatments. I cooked some of the meals in our cabin, and the ones I didn't cook, we went to that nice Italian restaurant she liked.

Kerry loves getting all 20 of her nails done the same color, so we had that done too. The hot tub in our room was also a nice touch so she could relax and forget the world. I know it was early, but it was a nice surprise for our anniversary.

I sang a song I had written for her, but hadn't shared yet. Previously the only song I had written for a girl was when I had broken up sadly. The song is called 'One Wish', and the words are as follows:

Just when I thought I had seen it all,
All the beauty in this world,
I walked through a door and there you were,
All I wanted in a girl
I never knew that I could smile this long
Till I first smiled at you

CHORUS:
If I were granted just one wish, I know what it would be.
I'd want to be the one to hold you tight, for all eternity

So tell me how to win your heart,
And I'll try to every day
When you're with me, I can do anything
My fears have flown away

CHORUS

Girl you'll always have my heart.
That's the way that it should be
It always hurts me when we're apart
So girl I hope you see

CHORUS

Chapter 15: 2005-2007

Kerry did seem to like the song just fine. She knows I am not always a details oriented kind of person, unless it has to do with football. Today though, she noticed that I had gone to great lengths to make our weekend away VERY memorable. After I sang to her, she looked into my eyes with that burning glow that melts me in seconds. That's where this journal entry can stop.

Chapter 16: 2009

Chapter 16: 2009

June 16, 2009

Today I received word that Eddy has been hired to coach the Lions football team next year. His agent has been trying to get him to do some positive public relations activities so his autobiography will sell better in the bookstores. Not only is Eddy coaching, but he has donated enough money to them to upgrade all of their equipment to more lightweight, sleek looking gear. The jerseys they wear will even be changing to something better. From what Hope said to me last year, I do worry if Eddy really had the money to be so generous. I hate that Eddy is working for my rival school. It may put strain on a friendship that has been not very great these last few months.

I wish Eddy well in his new job, but we are going to beat his team this year. The team I am coaching now is the fastest, strongest, smartest, largest group of boys this school has ever produced. Volleyball died out last year and was cancelled, so we got a few boys to return to where they should have been all along. No disrespect to volleyball, but this is a better way for things to be at our school. The football team provides more experience to more kids, and because of the grueling physical play, makes men out of boys in ways that volleyball just can't.

Brittney and Courtney have actually made the senior cheer team, which is quite amazing. They only turn 13 this summer, but the coaches wanted them on. That will be great because it will mean my girls can see every football game this season since they will be invited to ride the bus with the team for the away games. Kerry is a bit nervous about our little girls hanging around with kids (especially boys) so much older than they are. If I wasn't the football coach, I wouldn't have been comfortable with this arrangement either. Obviously, I will keep a close watch on my girls while they are with the team.

August 25, 2009

Confidence. That is the best word to describe the way my team feels heading into this football season. Before writing this, I glanced back at what I wrote on June 16th, and I think I understated how well this team performs their duties. They think the game so much faster. None of them have any obvious fears. My boys know their jobs very well, and they are secure enough to ask questions if situations make them unsure.

2nd Place

Any football coach will tell you that this physically demanding game is even more demanding mentally. Decisions, choices, and changed assignments all have to happen way ahead of the play. Minor mistakes can lead to huge problems. That's why for the last 5 years I have made a point of scouting the junior football games more, to see the boy's strengths long before they even come to my tryouts.

After years of fine-tuning my own coaching skills, I can say with confidence that every boy on my team is playing the right position, and seems to know his job, his limitations, and the flow of the game of football. Our first exhibition game last week was against the team that won the State Championship from a neighboring state. No one from our state has beaten a team from their state for 20 years.

That team came to our humble little field and expected to walk all over us. Maybe it was just as well that our new field won't be ready until the 2010 season. The swagger they had when they got off the bus was much like Eddy's. It was then that I knew we were going to win. Their overconfidence was going to kill them.

We scored on every possession. Some were touchdowns and some were field goals. We didn't allow them a touchdown. Just two field goals. We held them to less than 100 yards of total offence. We scored two punt return touchdowns. I put my rookies in after three quarters, and we still won 51-6. I don't agree with running up the score on someone else. When the rookie team scored the last three touchdowns, I didn't feel bad about that part though.

When the game ended, the other coach came to me to shake hands. That's pretty standard, but what he uttered wasn't. He asked, "Workman, whatever you are doing here, write it down in a book. I want to read up on your methods." I told him the short answer is to replace comparing, complaining and criticizing with being grateful, genuine, and gritty. He agreed about the gritty part, but was curious to know how the other two words fit with coaching.

To my kids who may not get to read this until after I die, I want you to know how this brief conversation with the other coach affected me. Humility is something my Dad taught me. Though my team dominated today, against what should have been great odds, I still don't think I am a better man than anyone else. The players play the games. I provide the best chance I can for them to succeed. My worry is that if I ever take glory to myself, I will somehow offend God, and my string of good fortune will end. Never in my coaching

Chapter 16: 2009

career have I felt like we had such a good chance of winning the State Championship as I do this year. I can't wait until we play the games that matter.

My starting quarterback this year is Andy. What a complete player. He can throw the ball hard, far, accurately, and no one can tackle him behind the line of scrimmage because he is too quick and too smart. His Dad, and I have become close friends these last few of years. Tony loves football, and comes to all of Andy's games. Tony still teases me about the mistakes I made when he was helping me finish our basement. Well, that's not true because the basement still isn't finished. Someday it will be.

Andy's Mother passed away 3 years ago in a car accident. That has made our friendship with Tony and Andy even more important. I can certainly relate to what Andy has gone through. I have had a few visits with him and have explained the grieving process I went through when I lost my own Mom at that age. Sharing a little bit of that with Andy seemed to give him permission to do the same thing. We all grieve in our own way, but I have told Andy the only thing he has to do for sure is to go through it, and come away with a resolve to be happy on his own terms and in his own time. Andy is closer to me than any of the players I have ever coached because of this.

September 4, 2009

Starting the season against the Lions seemed a little odd. It would have made more sense to play them later when we are both clicking, and in mid-season form. Far be it for me to complain though, as I must live by my own rules. Thrilling game tonight, but we played to a tie on our own field: 24-24. That old saying that 'a tie is like kissing your sister' seems to apply, though it is hard for me to relate to that because I only had brothers.

The way the game ended in a tie was a letdown. We were up by a touchdown, and it was only one freaky little wildcat play that beat us. Goofy little trick plays are not my style, but it looks like Eddy wants to coach that way, so we will have to keep an eye on the Lion's game films if we have to play them later on. The odds of that happening are pretty good because it appears the other teams in our league are not that great.

2nd Place

September 11, 2009

I hate this day. It reminds me of the terrorist attacks in NYC eight years ago. No matter. We beat the Falcons 42-5. We gave up a safety on the last play of the game just to be nice. They had fumbled on our 2-yard line on the second last play of the game. My rookies got lots of playing time, as we were ahead 35-0 by halftime.

September 18, 2009

Another game, another lopsided win. We crushed the Cowboys on their home field 59-10. I hope no one in school management ever reads this journal, but we were ahead by so much for so long, I found myself watching my little daughters on the cheer team more than ever. I love being a Dad, and I love my girls. The boys that date them better be good to them or there will be trouble.

September 25, 2009

This is getting too easy. My real concern now is to keep my boys from developing apathy or overconfidence. We played our rookies after the first quarter today and still won the game 76-0 against the Rams. By 10 minutes into the game, Andy had thrown three touchdown passes, and ran one in himself from 67 yards out. I can still remember the day the Rams beat us 56-4 three years ago. They kept their starters in all game. This was a pretty sweet turn around.

OK, it happened again. I was a little distracted by my daughters again today. They have been put in charge creating some of the cheers now. It's hard to write down what they do, but it is original, cool, and of course in good taste, because they are Workman girls. Their Mom is so proud of them. Kerry has started helping with the coaching side of the cheer team. My life is going so well right now. I have the best family a man could want. Still wish I had a son, but what I have will do, since it seems like what God wants me to have.

On the bus ride home, I visited with Andy to make sure he was not suffering too much from the lack of playing time the last two games. He is handling this very maturely. He understands we need to build for next year too, and that rookies should play a bit. We haven't ever had the luxury of resting starters this much. I hope this turns out to be a good thing on our way to a State Championship.

Chapter 16: 2009

September 29, 2009

Andy's life just got tougher. The strange new virus has made his father Tony very ill. I went to visit Tony in the hospital. We have had so many good times. Tony and I both like to go fishing and hiking. Hanging around with him and Andy on weekends has become a highlight for me these past couple of years.

Tonight, when I saw Tony, he looked so pale. He couldn't speak very loud, but he pleaded with me that if this illness took his life, that he wanted me to take Andy into my care, like my own son. I was honored by the invitation, but wondered why there wasn't family who could do that. Tony explained that he was an only child, and that Andy had no cousins, aunts, uncles, and that both sets of grandparents had passed away.

I agreed to Tony's request, but honestly felt that he'd recover, and this wouldn't ever need to happen anyway. I gasped when the next person who came into the room was a lawyer that Tony had arranged to sign legal documents to allow me custody of Andy. Doctors came in and out of the room quite often too. None of them could explain what was wrong with Tony. Tony must have known something was coming, as he died within hours of knowing Andy would be taken care of properly.

Stunned, I called Kerry on the phone and told her to come to the hospital. Everything happened so fast, and I regretted that I hadn't talked to her first before agreeing to help Andy this way. She got there in 10 minutes. We hugged each other and cried. Andy was brought in to see his Dad once more before they took his body away. Kerry and I both hugged him. He is such a tough kid, and hasn't been the type that was a hugger, but he was today.

If there was ever a woman who was prepared to do something this big for another person, it's Kerry. She has continued to take course work in counseling, and will most likely be the best thing that could have happened to Andy for now.

October 2, 2009

I left it up to Andy if he played or not today. He played the whole game. Made very few mistakes. I play him at linebacker too, and today he seemed to channel all of his anxiety into crushing our opponent.

We won 35-13 on the Cougar's home field. The game was

a secondary concern for my players and me. I am happy that we didn't lose, but it was beautiful to see my boys rally around their quarterback and team leader. The victory can't replace what he lost at home this week. Kerry and I have managed to make a bedroom for him downstairs. The first thing he hung up in his bedroom was a poster of Eddy Talent. The photo for it was taken when he still played for the St. Louis Rams.

I had to ask why Eddy was Andy's favorite player. All he could say was that Eddy was just so fast that he got into the heads of his opponents. Andy knows he is not as fast as that, but he does have an ability to unnerve his opposition by being so strong and determined to bring his 'A game' every night. He is physically tough and has so much endurance, and uses that to wear down other people. By the fourth quarter, he is just getting started when other players are ready to rest.

October 5, 2009

Today was hard for Andy at practice. He wanted to prepare for the next game, but his hands were shaking, and his throat was tight, and he was mentally not able to be with us. The funeral was two days ago, and I was surprised to see Andy at school at all today. I turned the rest of practice over to my other coaches, and I took Andy to our one and only burger joint in town.

I have not seen Andy cry much yet, but he did today. I cried too. My heart was broken for this boy. I have talked to Kerry for hours these last few days, hoping she'd be able to help me be the support Andy needs at this point. Her advice to me was to let Andy express everything he needs to. Kerry also suggested that my own experience with grieving over Mom's death when I was Andy's age probably would help him trust me somewhat since I would know his situation very well.

The last thing a grieving person needs is to be told to get over it when it is a loss they are suffering. The important thing to realize is that a grieving process must be complete first, and then life can and should go on in a healthy and balanced way. When ready, we must be willing to accept the fact that the person we have lost does not expect us to live unhappily with their memory. They will want us to be happy, and move forward when ready.

With all of this information about helping someone grieve

swirling around in my head, I let Andy talk through all he was afraid of. I told him he could choose to play the next game, or not. His team would understand either way. We just need him to be healthy. Andy said he wanted to play. He knew that somehow his Dad would still be watching, and would want him to do his best.

So, there we sat. Two men sobbing, knowing we were being watched over by a parent we couldn't actually see anymore. Andy thanked me for taking me into my home. He asked me to just listen to him whenever he needed it, and I promised I would always be there for him.

October 9, 2009

Today's home game against the Trojans was another victory. Andy played 3 quarters. He got 5 touchdown passes, 240 yards of passing, and ran for another 56 yards on sneaks and sweeps. The Trojans were actually very kind to him in the arm taps after the game. I overheard lots of them building him up, and complimenting him on playing the game of his life after his own personal loss. Yeah, I said 'arm taps'. The league doesn't want us shaking hands this year until H1N1 is a thing of the past.

November 6, 2009

I haven't written for a few weeks because I have been so focused on our games and preparation, and Andy's need to talk. He is such a smart kid too. I think he will be fine in life. He is already so grateful for what he still has. I don't know how he does this. If I were in his position, I would struggle and only be able to see what I had lost. Anyway, our first playoff game was successful last week. We also did very well again tonight.

We won convincingly and are prepared now to meet the Lions in the State Championship game. We have identical 7-0-1 records. The board of governors structured the playoffs so we would most likely meet in the final game, and they got their wish. That game is next weekend.

Andy has settled into quite a good rhythm of late. His timing is excellent, and he has gotten his commanding voice back in the huddle. The other boys will do whatever he asks of them. I am so pleased with him. I don't have a son of my own, so Andy is all I've got in that department. It is an honor to be like a Dad to him.

2nd Place

November 14, 2009

It is through tears I write today's journal entry about our game last night. It didn't go quite the way I thought it would. Before reading this, just be assured that everyone is OK in the end.

Eddy had the Lions ready to use every little trick play that could possibly be concocted. The Lions offence did some wildcat offence plays for most of the first quarter. We were off balance on defense for all of the first half, because we had not seen these plays. They were saving these plays for our game only, since the rest of the league was so weak compared to them and us.

Our offence continued to roll as it always had. The Lion's defense was the toughest one we faced this year, and we got 3 touchdowns on 5 possessions. The Lion's scored on all four of their possessions and had a punt return touchdown. They had a 35-21 lead at the half, and were also going to get the first possession for the second half.

Halftime speeches are not always so intense, but my guys on defense needed some serious encouragement to stick to our system no matter what the other team was doing in the backfield. Assignments do not change just because they are doing that stupid wildcat garbage. I encouraged my defense to gang tackle the ball carrier, except those with pass coverage assignments.

We decided to play exclusively a man-to-man pass defense and keep eight players in the box to stop all of the runs to the middle and the outside. Andy asked if he could play pass defense instead of linebacker because he knew he was fast enough. I did let him do that, and made some adjustments elsewhere. No one complained about the realignment. That was one moment where I was happy I had taught them to use gratitude to replace complaining.

In the second half, we started very strong. Our kick coverage had been good all game, except for the one touchdown, and the Lions started their first possession on their own 10-yard line. The new look defense stopped them on 3 straight wildcat plays that fell flat. I looked across at Eddy coaching on the other side. He was shrugging his shoulders a lot. I think our defense was getting to them mentally because it was their first three and out, and first punt of the game.

My hunch was right on. I asked Andy to be one of my punt returners instead of our usual player. The kicker put the ball to Andy's side. He caught the short kick in full stride, avoided one tackler, and scampered down the sideline for a touchdown. The Lion's kick coverage team was caught unprepared for the short punt, and overran the kick. Now the score was 35-28. We stopped the Lions on the next three possessions, but could only muster a field goal when we had the ball. Eddy has a pretty decent defensive co-coordinator too, we discovered.

With the score 35-31, we had the ball at the Lion's 49 yard line with about 2 minutes left to play. Andy mixed it up with run and pass plays well and with one minute left we had a first down on the Lions 3 yard line. I sent in a play action pass to put us into the lead for the first time all game.

The Lions countered with an all-out blitz that we weren't expecting. None of the Lions were fooled by the fake handoff, and they were about to smack Andy when he threw the ball toward our tight end. One of the lineman managed to tip the ball straight up just before a group of defenders hit Andy. His neck snapped back violently, and he went down heavily, and laid there motionless on the turf.

I forgot who I was for a few moments. While the Lion's ran the intercepted ball back for a touchdown, I was running onto the field screaming for no one to move Andy. I was so worried he had damaged his neck, and didn't want him to end up paralyzed for the rest of his life. Eddy could see the concern, and immediately got his players off the field so the medical team could attend to Andy.

He was in shock, and not very coherent. He wouldn't wiggle his toes or fingers like we asked. I asked the emergency medical team if I could accompany him to the hospital in the ambulance. We all agreed that he needed someone to talk to him and keep him conscious. I asked my assistants to take charge for me as I left. Right before leaving, I called a team huddle and told my players that I loved them all, that I was proud of them, and would be no matter what happened in the rest of the game.

Andy started to make more sense on the way to the hospital. He was awake enough to know where we were, and why he had been forced to leave the game. He asked if we scored the touchdown. Thinking his health was of primary concern, I told him we had so he would not worry. Then I told him his job was just to keep talking to me, but lie perfectly still. He said he could. I asked him to wiggle his toes, and he did. It hurt a little to do that though.

Andy does have a broken neck, but he is not going to suffer from being paralyzed. He will be in a neck brace for nearly a year, and won't be allowed to play any sports for at least that long. I stayed with him in the hospital over night. I called Kerry on her cell phone late last night to tell her how things were. She had taken the girls home with her after the game, since we knew Andy needed to be still and have no other visitors.

This morning I got a visit from Eddy. He knew I had a thing for a DQ Peanut Buster Parfait, and he brought one to the hospital for me. Not the healthiest breakfast, but it tasted good.

Eddy explained how the rest of the game had gone because I didn't get many details. My assistants had called me on the cell phone to say that we lost, and that the boys were pretty sad. They weren't allowed to visit Andy for the same reasons that Kerry and the kids were told to go home.

Eddy explained that my team had scored a late touchdown on the kickoff after the tipped ball, interception, and touchdown. It was not fancy, just great blocking, and determined running. They tried an onside kick to get the ball back because with 15 seconds they were still down 42-38. They successfully recovered the kick. They had two successful plays that got the ball down to the Lion's 24-yard line. With time for only one more play, they tried a pass to the end zone that didn't connect. The game ended 42-38 for the Lions.

Only Eddy could have shared the next part of the story. He told his players not to celebrate loudly. Yes, they had won, but out of respect for the game's biggest star, Andy, he thought it was more appropriate to be silent. Football is, after all, just a game. An injury can damage a life permanently. All of Eddy's players agreed that had Andy not been hurt, our team would have won the game. The only difference on the scoreboard was a fluke touchdown after the tipped ball.

November 15, 2009

Andy is sitting up in is hospital bed today. We should be able to go home later this week. Ralph Derrick has given me permission to stay here with Andy. He is covering all of my classes himself, or paying for sub teachers out of budgets that don't affect my personal one, or days off in my contract. Nice gesture. I guess he's not all bad.

Kerry calls me every six hours or so to see how Andy and I are doing. The girls miss me even though it's only been a couple of days. When Andy and I visited today, he asked me why I left the game to be with him. I explained that I was trained in university to know when an injury might lead to the athlete being paralyzed, and I couldn't sit by and let someone else mess things up.

Andy continued that he meant something a little different. He wanted to know not why I came, but why I left the football field when I had the possibility of all of my dreams coming true. It seemed a big sacrifice for me to leave at that moment. Someone else could have just as easily sat with Andy, talked to him, and been there for him.

I sat quietly for a moment. How could I answer that question? I didn't know. After a few moments of silence, I realized it was because I care about my players first. Greatness, accolades, trophies, glory are all a second priority. Players are not just pawns in a game I want to win. I have wanted to build men of greatness, because that is what teaching and coaching are actually about. I also explained how I felt concern for him personally, because I had promised his Dad on his deathbed that I would treat him like my own son. I did exactly that. I again uttered the advice I had given to Hope a few months ago. Since I considered Andy family now, it was fitting to tell him that no success can compensate for failure at home.

Andy then thanked me for meaning what I say, and saying what I mean. He said that the boys on the team talk about teachers and adults quite a bit. In their opinion, other adults 'talk the talk', but no one 'walks the talk' like coach Workman. I started telling him that I don't consider myself any better at that than other people. He interrupted, scolded me, and encouraged me to just shut up and accept the compliment. So, I did.

December 25, 2009

Our first Christmas with Andy was great. He still has the neck brace, but has most of his strength back, as he is allowed to go for a jog once in awhile. His neck is not fully stable yet, but the risks of damage to his spinal column are pretty much gone. Andy was very talkative though. He was a little teary-eyed as he spoke of the family traditions he used to have with his parents. Kerry and I agreed to add those traditions to our routine if he wanted. He told us to wait a year to do that.

We have noticed that Andy is the best big brother we could have asked for to watch over all of our girls. He protects Brittney and Courtney from thugs at school who take flirting too far to the point that it's downright rude. He has plans to go to university next year. His scores on entrance exams are excellent, and he has scholarships in place already for some of these places. He wanted to play football somewhere next year, but his injury may keep him away from that for the rest of his life.

Chapter 17: 2010

Chapter 17: 2010

February 26, 2010

Today, Derrick asked me to prepare a speech for the grand opening of the new sports field. This event is scheduled for March 27. The committee has chosen to name it after Eddy Talent. That seems fitting I suppose. The only hesitation I have is the fact that he presently coaches our school's biggest rival. The full name of it will be Eddy Talent Athletic Park. It's actually a cool little acronym. I have learned not to argue too much with administrators, and have already started preparing.

When Eddy played in the NFL, his way of celebrating touchdowns with his teammates was to tap helmets. He became known as 'E' and he gave 'E-taps' to people. So, yeah, this is a fitting way to immortalize the athlete from our hometown who has succeeded the most in the real world. His book sales for his autobiography have been pretty good. Last time I talked to him on the phone, he had sold around 20,000 copies. I am happy for him. The night Hope made a pass at me, I was very worried for Eddy. She seems to have changed her ways, and they appear quite happy now.

March 27, 2010

Spring is in the air. The grass is green, but no greener anywhere than what is on the new field. I can't wait until we play games there. We can comfortably sit three times as many people to watch games now because of the new stands on the west side. The last few years, many people have had to bring lawn and folding chairs.

My speech was typed up, ready to present, and I was sitting on the temporary stage at midfield. What a grand event for a small town like ours. I was just about to make my way to the microphone when Mr. Jones (Derrick) got up, and said that we were going to listen to a speech from Eddy first. Since it was his day, I didn't mind a little more time to sit back and get ready to say what I had planned. For the next part of my journal, I am going to insert the speech that Eddy gave, the speech that Derrick Jones gave, but first I will put my own here.

2nd Place

My Speech for Eddy March 27th

Good afternoon ladies and gentlemen. It is a great honor today for me to pay tribute to a man I've tried to keep up with for most of my life – Mr. Eddy Talent. My earliest memories of him were bittersweet. I never had a better friend. It was hard for me to lose every race to him, but he compensated for that by being good to me always.

Eddy is most noted for his tremendous success as an NFL player. He broke many long-standing records in yardage, catches, and touchdowns and was truly a force to be reckoned with throughout his career.

In our athletic program, we tell our athletes to be their very best, whatever that is. Ultimately, we all want that first place ribbon. Eddy is truly the model of what can happen when someone combines talent, effort, desire, and determination.

I will always remember Eddy's tremendous confidence. He always expected to win, and then simply went on his way and accomplished his goals. It is good to see him here today, and to learn again what his face really looks like, as I have seen him from behind most of my life, trying to keep up.

It is my great pleasure to honor him by naming our new field after him. Please join me in applauding our town's greatest athlete – Mr. Eddy Talent.

Chapter 17: 2010

Speech for field opening ceremonies – By Eddy Talent

Good afternoon ladies and gentleman. It is a great honor for me to come home today, and see this beautiful new field that our future generation can make memories on. It is amazing to me that a town this small can find the funding to build something so beautiful and complete, in an effort to provide an environment for your children to put forth their best efforts in athletics.

My good friend Rick Workman was asked to speak first at this event, as he has always been the most loyal of my friends. My speech today may surprise some of you because I am going to talk about Rick a lot.

There is only room at the top for one person to finish first in athletics. I was blessed with an ability to run fast. Naturally, I was able to beat most people I raced. Rick was the only real threat I faced here as a kid. He may not know that I toyed with him some days, while other times, I was terrified that my talent wouldn't be enough, and that his grit and determination would finally allow him to beat me. I had to raise my game to stay ahead of him. It was in doing that every year I raced Ricky that convinced me that my effort needed to improve. I am so grateful to him for pushing me like he did. I wanted him to succeed and be in the NFL with me, but that didn't happen.

I could tell that I was living his dream. I knew it would bug him if I rubbed it in that I was making in one year what he made in 10 or 20 years as a teacher and coach. It was Rick who stuck by me as a friend when a story hungry media tried to paint me as some sort of villain and public enemy.

On my visits here over the past few years, I loved seeing kids

2nd Place

playing football in parks, some wearing a jersey with my name and number on it. Every player who makes it to the big leagues remembers the joy of youth, the dreams of future greatness, of being that guy who makes a difference at the crucial part of the game. We all want the fans to cheer our name when the game is on the line.

Some of you may have read my autobiography by now. I got the impression that Mr. Jones hadn't read it when he approached me about naming this new athletic park after me. I praised Rick Workman in that book. He is the real champion on this stage today. I have known no one else so dedicated to his profession, to youth, to family, to community. I couldn't of good conscience let them name this field after me. I requested that they name this after Rick instead. After doing their homework on this fine man, my dearest friend, they agreed with me.

Thank you Rick for the difference you made in my life. Your students may have my posters on their walls at home, but they have you and your winning philosophies written on their hearts forever. With your permission Rick, I'd like to give the microphone back to Mr. Jones. Thank you to everyone who came here today.

Chapter 17: 2010

Speech for Rick Workman Athletic Park Opening Ceremonies – By Derrick Jones

Thank you Eddy. It is great to see you here today for this important event. Yes, we have good news here today. Part of my speech makes me look bad. There's no other way to say this, but I hope you will bear with me until I conclude.

I have known Rick Workman for almost 20 years. He has more than just taught here. He has built his players, his students, and his community in ways that other teachers can only dream of.

When I became his boss, I admit I didn't like him because I wanted results and first place banners. He had a reputation for getting to the big game and having his team fall apart. Early in my time here, I saw teams come so close to first place and lose. In my opinion, he was too soft, and didn't want to win badly enough. I made up my mind I would find a way to make him resign as football coach, because he was a volunteer and couldn't be fired from that responsibility.

I put pressures on him, assigned extra duties to make him too busy. I thought this school and community needed someone different as the football coach, and that they would finally have the championship season they had all worked for.

What happened next? Rick kept improving despite what happened. It turned out he wasn't soft at all, just gritty. Though his teams didn't come home with 1st place banners, they kept doing well, and many of Rick's players have played college football. This at a rate that other high school teams just can't match.

When Eddy Talent declined my request to name the field after him, I was quite surprised by that. Without hesitation he asked me to name it after Rick instead. I started doing homework on this man who has taught for me all these years. I called many of his former students who are now highly successful in their businesses and professions.

All of them were thrilled to hear about the honor I wanted to bestow upon him. Every one of them expressed their appreciation for the work ethic he showed and taught them. They have become successful people in their careers and feel it was Coach Workman who inspired them to develop the skills needed to be truly great in their lives. I have always been a win at all costs guy, but through the lives of his students, Rick shows all of us that winning can be defined in other ways.

Many of the students expressed concern, and asked how Rick was doing. They had heard stories about his house burning down, and the financial struggles he's had over the years, that were not necessarily his fault. With that in mind, it is my pleasure to introduce Mr. Kendon Smith, owner and CEO of his own internet marketing company.

Chapter 17: 2010

Speech for Coach Rick – By Kendon Smith

It is my great pleasure to ask that the covers be taken off the scoreboard so that Rick can see his name written there.

Rick, you have touched many lives in your career, and we want you to stay here until you retire. For this reason, I have assembled all of the successful college graduates you have ever coached to present you with a notice from your bank. We pooled our resources, and have paid off your mortgage for you. It was chump change for us to get this together for you and your dear wife, and your daughters.

A group of about 15 of us had dinner together two weeks ago, and we wondered what else we could do for you that would be even more meaningful and personal. I have in my hands the keys to a brand new Ford Mustang GT. You made it clear that this was your favorite car. (Toss the keys back to coach) There is a personalized license plate with the name Whitney on it. Many of us know the story about how much you were saddened by the passing of your little girl. We hope this gesture is a sweet reminder that her spirit lives on, and that she is so proud of her Daddy.

We also wanted to know what we could do for your wife. Behind every great man is a great woman, and

2nd Place

a surprised mother-in-law. After consulting with Mr. Jones, we determined that a new Home Ec. Room was in order, as that small place Kerry has suffered with all these years is not adequate for her needs. Again, I assure you that we are not going to be hurting after this donation of funding.

Congratulations Coach Workman. Not for what we have given you here today, but because we live well partly due to what you have taught us. We live by your creed about being genuine, gritty, and grateful. I won't mention the 'c' words, as we don't even keep them in our vocabulary anymore.

Many of you don't know how much Coach Workman helped me at a key time in my life. I will always remember his care and concern. But mostly, I will remember that he lives by the code he teaches. He helped me and my family put our lives back together when I was a high school student. I will forever be grateful for you, and for your dear wife for being there for me when I needed it most.

Coach Workman, may you have all your dreams come true, and may all future students enjoy having you at your best as the greatest coach and teacher we have ever known in our small town. Thank you for letting us all enjoy your big day with you.

Chapter 17: 2010

There is one more person who would like to speak here today. His name is Andy.

2nd Place

Speech for my Dad – By Andy

Many of you know that I played quarterback for Coach Workman's team for the past 2 seasons. He became a dear friend to my father and I during the last months of my Dad's life. I stand before you today grateful that I can walk. My neck was severely damaged in the last football game I ever played in, and I may not play football again.

I will always be grateful that Coach Workman left his post as head coach to make sure my trip to the hospital on that dark day was safe, and that in my weakened condition, that I was carried properly so no further damage was done to my body. He was so close to achieving his dream of coaching a championship team, but he left that all in a moment's notice to keep a promise he made to my Dad just before he died.

I miss my Dad. I miss my Mom. I know they live on somewhere. I can't see them, but I know they cheer for me always. I also know they want me to be happy now, and move forward with my life. It has been my honor to live in the home of Rick and Kerry Workman since my Dad died last fall. They have loved me like their own child. They didn't have to do this, but chose to anyway because I truly have no other family to turn to at this point in my life.

I feel it in my heart that I have my parent's permission to be a loving member of the Workman family. With your permission, I would like to call you Dad and Mom from here on, because that's who you have become to me. Thanks for showing me that family is most important, and that I am part of yours.

Chapter 17: 2010

March 28, 2010

Kerry and I went for a drive this afternoon in the new car. We told the kids we'd be back to take them for a ride later. I explained to Kerry about my chat with Eddy shortly after the ceremony was over yesterday.

Hope confessed to Eddy about what had happened the day she tried to get me to run off with her. She felt awful for her moment of weakness. They went for counseling together to keep their relationship intact. She came clean about the hidden money at a time when she and Eddy really needed it. Kerry was not previously aware of my crush on Hope from my teen years, but she was happy that I had made the right choice when faced with it.

My choice had made a difference in Eddy's life too. He knew he could trust me with anything. He thought my conduct demonstrated the ultimate in friendship in a moment when I could have taken everything away from him out of frustration or jealousy. He went to rehab for his drinking problem, and got to work on writing his book soon after.

After I got home from my drive, Kerry took the kids for the next ride in the Mustang. I sat on the back porch of my home – the one that is now paid for! While resting there, I watched some kids playing football on the field that is now named after me. I saw a future quarterback, receiver and defensive back with stars in their eyes. They were all dreaming of the day when they could play in the big game.

All the people who matter in my life were at the ceremony today. They all knew ahead of time about my surprise, and had our own family meal prepared to celebrate. Jennifer came up to me and gave me a big hug. She has been so good to me all these years, cheered for me, encouraged me on down days.

While I held her in my arms, I noticed Andy playing a card game with my girls in the living room. His kind words today had really touched me. I pulled back for a moment, and looked into Jennifer's face. I saw the love of a mother in her eyes. Once I got the lump out of my throat, I asked her if she would mind if I called her 'Mom' from now on.

She answered, "whatever you want coach Ricky." And then she held me close again, only much tighter. Just then, I noticed that Dad was close by. He gave me two thumbs up, and then went back to the kitchen to finish making the punch for our big dinner event.

After everyone had gone home, and my household was quiet because everyone was sleeping, I thought about the people who have helped shape my life. I can thank my parents and grandparents for a great legacy. I can thank my kids for a great future, and my wife for a great present.

I realized that Mom was right. There are very few people who are evil. Even if some of them oppose us in some way, everyone in my life has some good in them and I can learn from them. Yes, even Derrick Jones as it turns out. It took a lot of courage for him to say what he did today.

It was wrong of me to make him out to be some sort of villain. I know he had the student's best interests in his heart. He remembers well what it was like to win it all, and that's really all he wanted to see for my players.

At least one of my assistant coaches is not returning next year because his youngest son will be graduating from the 12th grade. I plan on asking Derrick to help coach football with me next year. If we still come in 2nd, he won't be able to blame me for that next time. Ha Ha!

Still finding it hard to sleep tonight, I reached for my Bible that mom had told me to read when I was little. I read John 14:2, and finally understood what it meant. The Lord has and is preparing a place for me. 2nd Place is still a place in His eyes, and I guess that is good enough for me.